DAYLIGHT SAVING

DAYLIGHT SAVING

EDWARD HOGAN

WALKER
BOOKS

First published in Great Britain 2012 by Walker Books Ltd
87 Vauxhall Walk, London SE11 5HJ

2 4 6 8 10 9 7 5 3 1

Text © 2012 Edward Hogan
Cover design © 2012 Walker Books Ltd

The right of Edward Hogan to be identified as author of this
work has been asserted by him in accordance with the
Copyright, Designs and Patents Act 1988

This book has been typeset in Cambria

Printed and bound in Great Britain by Clays Ltd, St Ives plc

British Library Cataloguing in Publication Data:
a catalogue record for this book is
available from the British Library

ISBN: 978-1-4063-3717-4

www.walker.co.uk

For Jesse and Alice and Emily

SUNDAY 21 OCTOBER

ONE

On the day we arrived, I thought I saved her life.

Dad drove slowly into Marwood Forest, home of Leisure World, Europe's biggest sports holiday complex, and – in my opinion – most colossal pit of hellfire.

"We just need to get away, Daniel," he said. "It's only for a week."

"A week," I said, shaking my head.

"It's not so long," he said. "We need some proper time together."

Time. It was all my family – or what was left of it – ever talked about. *In time, things'll get easier. We just need to put some time between ourselves and what happened.* Time apart. Time together. Time away from school.

"Besides," Dad said, smoothing his tracksuit top, "it's somewhere we can get healthy."

"I am healthy. There's nothing wrong with me," I said. I was a little sensitive about my weight.

Dad did that thing, where he puts his head back and then rubs his hand down the stubble on his neck. It was like he was strangling himself. He hadn't always done it. It was a new thing, like his obsession with growing vegetables, and crying. We pulled into the biggest car park I had ever seen. Metal and glass sparkled in the weak sunlight.

"I know there's nothing wrong with you, kiddo," Dad said. "It's me."

We got out of the car and started unloading our bags. Motor vehicles had to be left outside the complex; the brochure said that we would be transferred to our cabin in an "electric carriage". I could see one of them waiting by the Welcome Hut. It was an oversized golf buggy.

"I just think we need to get out in the fresh air. There's no air in our house," Dad said.

"There's no *TV* in our house," I said, and then wished I hadn't. It was true that Dad hadn't replaced the TV, but I was the one who'd destroyed it.

We began walking towards the electric carriage. Dad gripped his sports bag so tight that the blood drained out of his fingers, making the sprouting hairs look darker. He'd gone quiet, which was never a good sign.

"Dad?" I said.

"There'll be a TV where we're staying. I got us a Comfort Plus cabin. It's not quite as swish as the Executive but as you know, money is tight. Anyway, you won't need telly because there's every kind of sport you can think of, right here."

"I can think of about three," I said. "And I hate all of them."

We arrived at the carriage, and Dad gave the driver our cabin number and luggage, and turned back to me. "Maybe this week you'll find the sport you're really into," he said. "The one you're really good at."

I shook my head slowly.

"Well," Dad said. "There's a TV."

In the carriage, I rode up front with the driver – an old man with a grey beard – while Dad sat in the back with the bags. He tried to make light of the autumn wind blasting in through the open sides. "Welcome to the great outdoors!" he shouted, taking in a deep satisfied breath. I could see a Starbucks in the distance.

Leisure World was nature with a perimeter fence. A sports complex with shops and restaurants, set in the middle of the woods. Everybody stayed in wooden cabins, or wooden houses, or tall terraces, depending how rich they were, and families cycled past in tracksuits. There was so much nylon, and so much wood, that one match could have caused a fire you could see from space. There was a huge dome in the distance, a heated "tropical paradise" swimming centre with a wave machine and palm trees and rapids. I'd seen it in the brochure; it was Leisure World's centrepiece.

I never would have admitted it to Dad, but I felt a thrill of anticipation as we left the all-weather pitches and tennis courts behind and drove deeper into the forest. The shadows of the tall, planted pines darkened the inside of the carriage, and I thought I heard a long low hum. You could forget –

if you tried – about the plastic nonsense of Leisure World, and concentrate on the dark heart of the woods. You knew that when the light fell, the creatures would wake. You knew that in a thousand years, when every single one of these happy holiday families was dead and buried, nature would take this place over again. Ivy would cover the little cabins, and the thick roots of trees would burst through the floors. Eventually the water in the Tropical Dome would turn green, and fish would reclaim the Jacuzzi. There'd be screaming birds in the palm trees, and foxes looting the store cupboards, trotting through the restaurants.

"Daniel!" shouted Dad. "You haven't seen the plant food, have you?"

He had his head down, rummaging around inside bags, looking for nutrition for his beloved tomato plant. I didn't answer, because a girl had stepped out into the middle of the road. She wore a red hooded top over a swimming costume. Her hair was bedraggled and wet. I looked at the old man driving the carriage and waited for him to slow down. He didn't, and the girl didn't move.

"Aren't you going to…?" I said to the driver.

"What?" the driver said.

We were five metres away when I grabbed the wheel and dragged it to the left. We missed the girl by centimetres, but we crashed through a wooden barrier, and the carriage flipped onto its side. My world tumbled and I smacked my head against the dashboard. When the carriage came to a rest, I was on my back, looking up at a giant oak. The driver had landed on top of me, and he was less than happy. "What the bloody hell do you think you're doing?" he said.

"What were *you* doing?" I said. "You nearly ran that girl over."

"What girl?" he shouted. I climbed out from under the driver and stood, looking out onto the road. There was nobody there but Dad, shaking his head and nursing his tomato plant.

TWO

"What was that about, Daniel?" asked Dad as we walked the rest of the way to our cabin.

"The bloke was about to run over a girl," I said.

"He reckons there wasn't anyone there," Dad said.

"Who are you going to believe?"

"Well, given your recent track record—"

"What? Oh thanks."

"Look, lad, that's just the sort of behaviour I was hoping you might avoid on this holiday. You could've killed the old bloke, pulling the car off the road like that. You could've killed all of us."

"It was a *golf buggy*. Nobody dies in a golf buggy crash."

I thought back to the girl on the road. Faint wisps of steam had risen from her shoulders. I'd had hallucinations before. It was all part of the behaviour Dad was hoping I would avoid. But he had his behaviours, too, since Mum left. They mainly revolved around the Star and Sailor pub, where he would play the Who Wants to Be a Millionaire video game, drink nine pints of bitter and then come home with a broken nose and chilli sauce down his shirt. Cutting loose, he called it.

We arrived outside our Comfort Plus cabin. It was small and dark, overhung by a sprawling cedar. There was one big window and one small. It looked like someone had punched our cabin in the face.

As we were taking the bags inside, two women in tennis gear cycled onto the drive of the cabin next to ours. They were a bit younger than Dad, both with the same springy curls, and broad smiles. Sisters. Dad was carefully lifting the cherry tomato plant from the ground. I was a bit embarrassed that he'd brought it in the first place, so to see him publicly talking to the plant as though it were a baby was mortifying.

"Welcome to Leisure World," one of the women said to me, grandly. She was being sarcastic.

"You know you can never leave," the other one said. "This is Chrissy and I'm Tash."

Chrissy was shorter, and had a little grey in her hair. The younger one, Tash, wore more tightly fitting clothes, and an expensive-looking bracelet.

"I'm Daniel," I said. I looked at Dad but I really didn't know what to say, because he was fondling the tomatoes like the pearls of a priceless necklace.

"I'm Rick," he said, without looking up. He'd only been calling himself Rick for about a month, and it still made me wince. He used to be Richard.

"Hello," Tash said. "Have you been here before?"

"Nope," Dad said.

"It's our first time, too. We've come here to get in shape." She said it with a smile, and it seemed blatantly obvious to me that she was fishing for a compliment, because they were both thin as rakes. I waited for Dad to say so.

"Right," he said.

"What brings you to Leisure World, then?" asked Tash.

Dad held the plant pot above his head and studied the base. "We just needed to get away from things," he said. "At home."

"Oh," said Chrissy. "I see."

I felt the atmosphere become awkward.

"It's for the tomatoes, really," I said. "They haven't had a holiday in ages."

Both women laughed loudly, and Chrissy put her hand on my arm. "Bless you," she said. "Listen, if you need anything, or you fancy a game of doubles, do come over and give us a knock."

"Thanks," I said, because Dad wasn't saying anything. "Do you know anywhere good for food?"

The sisters looked at each other. "There's all the usual places, of course, but actually I like the Pancake House down by the beach," said Chrissy.

"It's not really a beach, Chrissy," said Tash, laughing.

"OK," said Chrissy. "There's a restaurant called the Pancake House on the bit of imported sand near the manmade lake. Or you could just come to our house to eat. We're doing an autumn barbecue."

Tash pointed to the tomato plant. "You guys could bring the salad."

"The Pancake House sounds fine," Dad said, taking the plant inside. I followed him in.

"Bye," they said.

"Bye," I replied.

Dad had started growing vegetables soon after Mum left, but the tomato plant was his pride and joy. It was the first plant he bought after she'd gone, and was too precious to leave at home. "The taste of the Mediterranean," he always said. This from a man who could only afford to take his holidays in Nottinghamshire.

He put the tomatoes by the kitchen window, and placed a couple of shaving mirrors around the plant, to reflect the sun. Then he took out a baby bottle full of rainwater that he'd collected at home and began to squirt the ripe, full fruits. "You give love and attention to a plant like this," he said, not for the first time, "and it gives you everything it's got in return."

He had driven all the way in Havaianas with socks underneath, and now that he'd taken off the flip-flops, there was a groove in his socks by his big toe that made his feet look like hooves.

"They seemed nice," I said.

"Who?" he said.

"Those women. The neighbours."

"Lesbians," he said.

"Dad, they were sisters!"

He shrugged. "And by the way," he said. "There's no need to be making public wisecracks about the tomato plant, thank you very much. There's such a thing as family loyalty, you know, although I don't suppose…"

He trailed off, and I knew it was because he was about to say something about Mum, or even about me. I wished he would. Anything was better than that fake smile. The smile said: "It wasn't your fault, lad." Which, of course, meant that it was.

I looked around the cabin – a lot of fake wood, a few stiff sofas with enough jazzy designs to hide the stains – while Dad got the rest of the stuff from the car. I figured the TV was hidden in one of the cabinets. Leisure World guaranteed a soundproof sleep (everybody likes nature, but you don't want it to wake you up), and so when Dad closed the door, the airtight seal made a sucking noise, and I felt my eyes pop out by a centimetre.

"Right," he said, looking at his watch. "We'll go and get our bikes, pop into the Tropical Dome for a quick splash, and then see if we can't find this Pancake House, eh? Brilliant."

THREE

So, you didn't drive at Leisure World, but you didn't walk either. You cycled. If you were a little boy, you rode a BMX. If you were a full-grown man, you got a mountain bike. People of my size had to ride a "Shopper", which is a woman's bike – white and pink, with no crossbar and a basket on the front. To be honest, I had almost given up on looking anything other than an idiot. "Can't I have a BMX?" I asked.

"That's a kid's bike," Dad said.

"Health and safety," said the bike man.

"He needs all the health and safety he can get, this one," Dad said to the bike man. "He's a danger to himself and others."

That was a quote from the incident report the school had sent. The bike man appraised me with a new respect.

We took the bikes, and cycled away like husband and wife.

Some part of the dome was always in view, and now, as we rode, we saw the trees peeling back to reveal it. It loomed huge above us. The shell of the dome was made from giant hexagons of reinforced plastic, and you could see inside. We stopped our bikes and watched kids deliriously throwing themselves down the water slide into the "rapids" – a stretch of moving water. I'd been off school for the previous fortnight, but it was half-term now, so there were lots of other kids about. It was weird to be around people my own age again. Men moved along the rapids in a long line like a supermarket queue; they seemed serious and purposeful as the current carried them along. I looked at their faces and – of course – I looked at their bodies. Real palm trees hung over the fake rocks by the edge of the water. You could hear the dull sound of screams from inside.

"I'm hungry," I said.

"Surely not," Dad said. "It's only six. Let's get in there and work up a proper appetite. It looks great."

"I don't really feel like swimming."

"You don't have to swim. Look. There's loungers." Dad pointed to an area of wooden decking, where a group of boys in swimming shorts were talking to two girls in bikinis. The girls were drinking milkshakes through straws and trying not to laugh.

"You could just sunbathe," Dad said.

"I can't *sun*bathe," I said. "Because the sun is *outside*."

"It's a constant twenty-nine degrees in there."

"It's warm enough out here," I said, although it was pretty cold.

"Is this how it's going to be, Daniel? For the whole holiday?"

I looked away.

"Most kids would give their right arm to be here. God, it's not like I'm asking you to take your top off."

"Dad, Jesus," I said. There were other families cycling by.

"Even if you did, nobody would look at you," Dad said.

He stopped talking then. I stared down at the T-shirt stretching across my soft body. Thinking back, he probably meant it in a nice way. He was probably trying to say that people are too busy getting on with their lives to tease a kid with a bit of extra weight. But there were two problems with what he said: firstly, I knew from experience that he was wrong. People *do* look. They *do* notice. Secondly, what kind of a state was I in, where the best thing I could hope for was that people wouldn't look at me?

"I'm going back to the cabin," I said.

I turned the bike around and began to walk away, but I could feel the full weight of his sadness behind me. Even though it was *me* that should have been upset, I knew that something like this could set him off. He might cry for a week or – even worse – drink.

So. I turned back.

He had his head in his hands. His feet were rooted to the floor, and the bike leant between his legs. "Dad," I said.

"Yes."

"Can we just go to the pancake place? Maybe I'll feel like swimming tomorrow."

I waited for a moment. Eventually he took his hands away from his face. There was that smile again. Sadder than anything I'd ever seen.

"Course we can, Daniel."

FOUR

The Pancake House was like one of those diners they have in American movies. It was a curved white building, with big windows that stretched all the way around, giving customers a good view of the lake. It stood on the fake beach, and I could feel the sand seeping into my trainers as we walked the bikes over.

The sight of the lake was calming. I felt my temperature drop as I looked out across the water, and my heartbeat slowed. One. And. Two. And. Three. And.

There were only a few boats still out, and most of them were making their way into the little wooden harbour. I could almost feel the plummeting depths of the water in my stomach. The lake was surrounded by trees, and you could hardly see the other side, just a few lights coming on in the cabins out there. There was a sign on the beach: STRICTLY NO SWIMMING. Sounded like a TV programme.

"Come on then, if you're coming," Dad said, opening the door.

The Beach Boys played on the Pancake House stereo. "Everybody's going surfing, eh, Daniel?" Dad said. "Everyone but us." He gave me a little punch on the arm, which made a slapping noise. It was a little bit too hard to be playful.

I ordered a cheese and mushroom crêpe, and a cherry and ice cream pancake to follow. Dad asked for a burger, and a maple syrup pancake for dessert. "Do you serve beer?" he said to the waiter.

"We've got a fully licensed bar, sir," the waiter said, gesturing to the spirits on the back shelf.

"Wow. It's great in here. Those lezzers were right," Dad said.

"Pardon, sir?" said the waiter.

"Nothing. I'll have a bottle of your finest lager, if you please."

I had mixed feelings about the bar. It meant that Dad might not force me to go to the Tropical Dome, but it also meant I might be carrying him back to the cabin at the end of the evening. Maybe he wouldn't drink so much on holiday, I thought.

Five beers later, he started going on about Mum again. "I'm not blaming anyone," he said. "Least of all…" he pointed to me. "Not anyone."

I looked at the leftover pancake on his plate. It was like a blotchy roll of fat. I picked it up and ate it in one go, just so I didn't have to look at it any more. Thankfully, Dad stopped talking for a second.

"Don't you think you've had enough?" he said.

"Don't you?" I said, looking at his empty beer glass.

He followed my gaze. "Oh. I appear to be without a drink. Waiter! Another of your finest, if you please."

He always used this ridiculous posh voice when he was on the ale. I could see why people might punch him on the nose.

It was getting dark now. I looked out of the big windows at the lake, which held a little of the moonlight on its surface. The water was lapping over the sand. I followed the ripples out into the middle of the lake, and thought I saw a disturbance there, a figure cutting the surface of the water, gliding towards the bank in the distance.

I closed my eyes and took a few deep breaths. I'd had hallucinations at school, just before I'd lost it. They'd given me a "little break", then. But now I was on holiday. Where did they send you when you flipped out on *holiday*?

Out on the lake, I was pleased to see that the water had stopped rippling, and there were no figures on the horizon. *Thank God*, I thought.

The Pancake House was converting itself into a winter beach cafe. People were sitting outside at tables under big outdoor heaters, trying to pretend it was summer but smoking to keep warm. Inside, a group of men and women mingled at the bar. Dad looked over at them, nodding his head to the music, not quite getting the rhythm.

"Dad, I've got a headache," I said.

"Oh, yeah?" He looked pleased. "Well, you should go home, Daniel. I mean, to the cabin. You don't want to be hanging around here with your old man. Not if you've got a headache."

"Are you staying then?" I asked.

"Yeah, I'll just stay for another of their finest. A little nightcap. You've got to, erm, you know..."

"Cut loose?"

"Aye, that's it. Cut loose."

I stood up from the table, and so did Dad. We walked in opposite directions, him towards the bar, me towards the door.

"Oh, Dad," I said.

"Yes, Daniel." He turned, sipped from his drink.

"Don't drown," I said.

He laughed. "I shan't be going in the lake," he said.

I nodded to his beer. "I'm not talking about the lake," I said.

Outside the air was cool and crisp; autumnal. I unlocked my bike from the stand. None of the drinkers outside seemed to notice that it was a woman's bike. Maybe Dad was right. Maybe nobody was looking.

I could see the cycle path as I walked my bike along the beach. The bicycles had dynamos, which meant that when you pedalled, your light came on. The dynamos made a clicking sound, like grasshoppers. Each of the cabins had two little posts on the lawn, with a lamp inside. These were the only sources of light. With the clicking of the dynamos, the weird white lamps and the cyclists sweeping their beams across the forest, it looked like an underwater planet.

I glanced back out to the lake. My eye was drawn up to the higher branches of a tree, where I saw a figure lying along a bough, wearing a bright red top with the hood up, and one leg hanging down. It was the girl from the road. I shook my head, and turned to the people sitting outside the Pancake House. They talked and smoked, stared into each other's eyes. They hadn't seen the figure. Perhaps I hadn't seen it, really.

I took a deep breath and looked back out to the tree. The distant figure was still there. I closed my eyes and turned away.

FIVE

Back at the cabin, I opened the TV cupboard and turned on the set. There were lots of satellite channels, but most of them were showing sport, so I turned it off again. For a moment, I thought I saw shapes on the blank screen. I thought I could see that tree out by the lake, with the figure sitting in it like a leopard. I rubbed my face. *I'm just tired*, I thought. I shut the doors of the cupboard.

I listened carefully to the silence in the cabin. I listened until the silence fell away and revealed the noise of Chrissy, Tash and their friends laughing in the garden next door. Their barbecue must have been winding down. I could smell the charred food. Beyond those sounds, I could hear the forest, its rhythms and night murmurs. I could almost feel it pressing in on the cabin.

I went to bed and lay awake for a while, thinking about what had happened back home, with my mum. Thinking about time. When they tell a story, a lot of people say, "I don't know where to start." I know what they mean.

*   *   *

I could start at 2 p.m. on the fourth of September. The day after the first day back at school. I was at home watching TV. Our house shares a sheltered entrance with the off-licence next door. It's like a little corridor. The off-licence put a security camera by the entrance, and weirdly, if you went to the second AV channel on our TV, it linked up to the camera. I used to switch it on sometimes when I heard people downstairs. The problem was, you couldn't leave it on too long because it would burn the image on to the screen. I don't know why. It was a technical thing. Our TV was pretty good. A nice Samsung, quite new.

At 2 p.m., on the fourth of September, I heard a noise downstairs. I wasn't expecting anyone, and it wasn't in my interests to have company when I was playing truant. So I hit AV2 on the remote to see who it was. It was Mum. She was just inside the alleyway, by the entrance. And she was kissing a man. I recognized him. It was Dr Greggs, our local GP. The kiss was a passionate one; he had his hand inside her coat, around her waist. All this was happening in black and white, on our telly. I was paralyzed, and only managed to snap out of it when I heard a sizzling noise coming from the TV. I switched it off and went up to my room. Thankfully Mum came in alone, and by the time she realized I was in the house, she was more concerned about the nosebleed that had forced me to come home from school.

For the next few days, I was rigid was fear. We were sitting there, in the living room, watching TV, and over the top of the moving pictures, I could see the scorched image of my mum and Dr Greggs kissing. Nobody else seemed to notice. I suppose you had to be looking for it in the first place, but it was clear to me. I could see the shadow of their kiss over Match of the Day, over the six o'clock news, over kissing couples in the films my mum watched. It was driving me mad.

Eventually, at about 3 a.m. one morning – when any old thing seems like a good idea – I woke up, got dressed, unplugged the TV, and walked out of the house with it. It was frosty and calm on the street. I was going to throw it in the brook and fake a break-in. I thought everything would be OK, I thought I was going to get away with it. But Mum had heard me close the door, and she opened the upstairs window. "Daniel?" she called down.

"Yes, Mum," I said.

"Are you awake?"

"I don't know," I said, resting the TV on my thigh.

"Come on back in the house, love," she said.

I shook my head. Mum leaned back inside the curtains, and I could hear her coming down. I could still see the picture branded on the TV screen, her shape the colour of milky coffee, with a dark orange outline. Him, too. Greggs. Greggs who had rubbed my neck in a circular motion when I had a suspected throat infection. Greggs, with his warm hands. Mum arrived at the door, smiling, in her dressing gown. "Come on, love," she said.

I walked back towards the house and dropped the television, screen first, onto the little wall of our front garden, denting and crumpling the screen. I made it look like an accident.

* * *

For a while, my parents were so distracted by my behaviour that they didn't have time to think about anything else. They whispered about what might be wrong with me, and sent me to the doctor (not Greggs) to talk about sleeping patterns and the need for exercise and fresh air. They sent me to a school counsellor, who asked me about friendship groups and the pressure of schoolwork, and issues of sexuality. It was easy to pretend that I was upset about such things.

Dad picked me up from school one day, and pulled over on the way home. I was expecting more of the same questions. Perhaps a talk about how it was perfectly OK to get pleasure from my own body, or that people were often a little plump during their teens.

"Did you see your mother with another man?" he asked.

He looked at me when he said it. I could feel him reading my features. And I knew they were telling him a story. There was nothing I could do. I didn't even say anything, but my face told him everything he needed to know. I hated him for looking at me like that. Hated myself for not being able to control how I looked. Hated how easy it was. Mum was gone by the next day.

But you could start that story earlier. You could start it from my nosebleed in history class, which meant I had to go home. Or you could start with the boys reading back the letter I sent to Lauren Harket over the summer holidays, which caused me to give myself the nosebleed. It wasn't the first time I'd done that, either. I'd worked out that if I used a nasal spray for hay fever at five times the recommended dose, a crust formed in my nostril, and when I picked that crust, *bang*, there's your bloody nose and a free pass to get out of school. So you might start the story from there.

Then again, why would anyone spend months preparing their nose so they could make it bleed whenever they wanted to? I certainly didn't have hay fever in September. Maybe it was because the boys who had read the Lauren Harket letter in high-pitched voices had also, a few months before, used Photoshop to put my head on the body of a toddler from a nappy advert, and a naked model from a website called BigBeautifulWomen.com. And maybe they had done that because, just after Easter, Sarah-Jane Kennedy had called me "toddlerbody" after seeing me at the swimming pool, and someone had offered to buy me a bikini top.

And why stop with me? I can remember Mum and Dad talking in the living room back on Valentine's Day. "Let's have a dance, Richard," she said to Dad. "We used to dance all the time."

He hadn't wanted to, but she convinced him. They tripped over a stray sofa cushion and Mum fell awkwardly. Three days later she went to see Dr Greggs. It was the first time she'd been to the doctor since we'd moved to the area. I don't need to tell you what happened next.

And Mum said that the problems with Dad started a long, long time ago.

So:

- The sofa cushion
- The TV

- The Photoshop pictures, and the chair I threw at the boy who had made them
- The security camera
- The Lauren Harket letter
- The hay fever medicine, which smelled of flowers, and reminded me of summer even in the sludge of October.

I didn't. Know. Where. To start. People always said to me, "You can't do anything about it, now." But when I looked back at all the little things that led to me destroying my family, I didn't know if I could have done anything about it *then*, either. It doesn't make it any easier, being powerless.

MONDAY 22 OCTOBER

SIX

I woke early. It must have been the noise of Dad going to bed. I could hear muffled voices. I was still dressed, so I got up and walked through to the "living area". It was a mess. There were beer bottles on the table, and the contents of Dad's rucksack – his swimming shorts, his towel, his shaving bag – were strewn across the floor. The muffled voices were coming from the TV. Dad had tried to watch the Sex Channel, but it was scrambled. I could just make out the bodies behind the grey fuzz, and hear their fake cries of pleasure. They sounded angry. I looked closer at the television, and saw Dad's dusty footprint spread across the edge of the screen. It was 5 a.m.

I walked out into the forest. The little lights were still shining from the lawns, and they looked like sprites between the trees. The sky was like the metal hull of a great ship. It was so quiet I could hear the generator from the Tropical Dome, and the street sweepers somewhere, cleaning up nature.

I took the Shopper out towards the lake, its dynamo clicking away as I pedalled. The mist was heavy above the water. The Pancake House looked menacing now it was empty. Inside, the stools were upside down on the tables. I noticed for the first time the green filth at the base of the white walls. *Good*, I thought.

I stood on the edge of the "beach" and watched thin ripples break on the sand. The water in the lake was too dark for a reflection, too cloudy. Suddenly I felt exposed out there. I felt as though I was being watched. So I took the bike off-road into the trees, and cycled alongside the lake.

I heard a noise from the water. It was a gliding sound so similar to the rhythm of my cycling that for a while I didn't even register it. But then I stopped the bike and looked out. It was difficult to see through the trees, but there was a figure cutting beneath the surface of the lake. I saw the way the water dragged behind the swimmer like the train of a long dress. I waited for the figure to come up for air. It took a long time, but eventually, she did. *She*.

It was the girl.

They say all people look the same in the water, but I now knew that wasn't true. At the local baths back home, they taught us to swim fast, to race, our arms thrashing and legs turning up white spume, while we took desperate gulps of air. But this girl swam like she was asleep. Even from that distance I could see that her eyes were half open when she came up to breathe, and she barely parted her lips before sinking back into the brunt, her body rippling like the water. She did front crawl with this slow, familiar rhythm.

One. And.

Two. And.

Three. And.

A waltz. Her arms were strong and long and came over her head with such silent grace I could barely hear them slipping back under. She wore a black swimming costume. My mouth was dry. I was too far away to see the details of her face when it finally emerged again.

Without really thinking, I carefully lowered the bike to the ground and crept a little further towards the bank, walking alongside her route. I followed her like that for five minutes, watching the steam from her body and the steam from the water rise up into the mist. She was the only smooth thing in that foggy world.

I saw some clothes in a sandy clearing on the bank, and tucked myself in behind a tree, getting so close that the bark grazed my cheek.

She began to make her way towards the bank, and without a stumble she was on her feet, walking through the shallows, shedding the water, smoothing back her hair. Her shoulders and hips were broad, and the swimming costume shone like oily seal-skin.

She picked up the red top from the ground, and I knew she was the figure I had seen in the tree the night before. I was surprised to see her zip the hoody straight over her wet self. She shuffled into a short jean skirt. Denim. It felt like I hadn't seen denim for years.

I was about twenty metres away now, and I looked back at

the Shopper, which was out of sight in the undergrowth. The girl walked up the bank a little way and sat down with her back against a tree. I was still hidden from her. She stared out onto the water and so did I. It rocked slightly with the memory of her body. She sighed, and I thought it was a sigh of peace and satisfaction. "I suppose," she said into the air, "it might be awkward if you came out now."

I looked around, desperately hoping she was talking to someone – anyone – else. She carried on. "Eh? I mean, you could pretend to be doing bark rubbings, or looking for your lost dog or something, but I think we both know what's going on."

She aimed a sly glance over her shoulder, in my direction. "Come on," she said. "Out you come."

I stepped out from behind the tree, my pulse slamming so hard it rocked my vision. She turned to look at me. I couldn't say anything.

"The thing is," she said. "You can go online, and very easily be looking at *fully naked* women within two minutes, with no trees to obscure the view."

I shrugged. "We're in a Comfort Plus cabin," I said. "It's all my dad could afford. No Wi-Fi."

She laughed and smoothed her hair back. "That wasn't really my point," she said.

"I thought you might be … in danger, in the water," I said.

"No, you didn't," she said, looking out onto the lake again. She was right. I'd never seen anyone look less in danger.

Her face was sharp and angular, the skin cold and white. There was a faint rim of green around her right eye. I couldn't tell if it was eyeshadow or a fading bruise. She wore one of those big digital G-Shock watches, with underwater capacity. She looked me up and down. "What's your name?" she asked.

"Daniel."

She stood up. "Right then, Daniel. Get 'em off," she said.

"What?" I said.

"Come on. Chop-chop." She motioned up and down with her finger.

"I don't understand," I said.

"Your clothes, Daniel. Take them off. You've had a good look at me, now let's have a gander at you. Strip."

There were lots of reasons why I didn't want to do that. One of them was that I had a raging hard-on. "I can't," I said.

"Don't make me come over there and do it for you," she said. This did not help matters.

"Really," I said. "I can't."

"Do it. Otherwise it's not fair. You've seen me in my cozzie."

I was trembling as I pulled off my sweatshirt. She looked away. The steam was still rising off her shoulders and the drenched curls of her hair. I could see faint red marks on her left leg, a rash from the water, maybe.

I couldn't take my T-shirt off. I kept thinking about school, about the pictures. Toddlerbody. For a horrible moment, I thought I was going to cry. She must have sensed my hesitation because she turned to look at me again. "Oh God," she said. "I was only messing around. You don't have to. Sorry."

I picked up my sweatshirt and pulled it back on. I was angry.

"Why don't you sit down?" she said.

I shook my head.

"It's nice, that T-shirt," she said quietly. It was just a light blue T-shirt, nothing special. "It looks good on you."

I sat down. "How come you can swim so well?" I said.

"People think you have to thrash around to swim well, but it's not true. The average dolphin is eighty per cent efficient in the water."

"The average dolphin?" I said.

"Eighty per cent of its energy goes into propelling it forward. Guess how efficient the average human is."

"I don't know. Fifty?"

"Fifty! Way off. Three per cent. Three per cent efficient. Ninety-seven per cent of their energy is wasted."

"Right."

"Swimming's easy," she said. "You just make a wave, and ride it."

We sat for a moment, watching a heron on the far side of the lake, his crown feather like an old man's comb-over gone awry. We listened to the park waking up behind us. One of the staff started checking the boats over by the harbour.

"You must have good eyes," she said.

Not as good as yours, I thought. They were brown and green, dizzying.

"Why?" I said.

"You saw me, the other day. When you were in the electric carriage."

"I knew it was you! I saved your life."

"Not sure about that, Daniel. And you saw me last night.

When you were in the Pancake House."

"It's not that far away. You were wearing a bright red top. There was a sign that said *No Swimming*, but you were swimming."

"Well. Not many people see me."

"I'm glad I did," I said.

"Steady on. Don't give your heart away, yet."

I turned away because I could feel my face going red. I put the sweatshirt over my moobs. "You know, I was only looking at you, because—"

"Because you wanted to. Because you're a boy and you can't help it. It's in you," she said.

"What's *in* me?"

"The darkness. The will to do bad things if you can get away with it."

"I don't think—"

"All you boys. And men. You've got all this hate and anger and desire, and when you're faced with the temptation of a woman, you can't help yourselves."

"Hate? It's not hate. I don't believe that."

"Believe what you like. It's your nature."

"Are you religious?" I said.

"Not any more," she said.

"What's your name?" I asked.

"Lexi," she said. She extended her fist, and I knew she was being sarcastic. I laughed. "Come on," she said. "Touch the glove."

I looked down at her hand, and the big watch on her wrist.

Something made me uncomfortable, but I couldn't work out what it was. "It's very nice to meet you, Daniel. You're very interesting, and you have excellent eyesight."

"I have to wear glasses for reading," I said.

"You have excellent *mind*sight, then."

I put my fist against hers, slotted my knuckles into the gaps.

She seemed to signal that the meeting was over, so I stood up and started walking towards the Shopper. I turned back, and looked again at the yellowy colouring around her eye. "When... How can I see you again?" I said. "Where will you be?"

"I'll be here," she said. "But no peeping from behind the trees, OK?"

SEVEN

Dad wasn't there when I got back to the cabin. Sometimes he couldn't cope with the shame of a hangover. He wasn't shamed enough to tidy up though. I went through to the kitchen area (there are no real rooms at Leisure World, only "areas") and picked up my rucksack. Dad had watered the tomato plant. But I noticed something strange about it. Four or five of the tomatoes had a green tinge to them. My life at home, with its guilty televisions and deliberate nosebleeds, was beginning to look normal compared to Leisure World. I checked that my swimming kit was still in the rucksack, and I left the cabin.

Chrissy, the older of the two sisters, was out in the garden next door, putting last night's leftovers in the bin. "Hey," she said. "Daniel. Wait up."

I stopped. "Hi," I said.

She crept close to where I was standing with the bike. "I wanted to talk to you."

"OK," I said.

"Your dad," she said.

"Oh," I said.

"He came over to the barbecue last night."

Maybe, I thought, *he went to the barbecue, drank a cup of tea, and told a funny and charming story. Maybe not.*

"He seemed a bit ... the worse for wear. Was he OK when he got home?"

"Fine."

"Does he usually drink like that?" she asked.

"Everybody needs to cut loose once in a while."

She smiled and her shoulders dropped. "He reminds me of my ex-husband," she said. "Running too fast because he thinks he might be able to get away from himself."

"I've got to go," I said.

"You know, you seem stressed out, Dan. I practice Reiki. It's basically a way to relax. A bit like massage. Maybe I could book you in for a session."

"I've got to go," I said.

I grabbed the Shopper and left.

I didn't really know why I was going to the Tropical Dome. I had forgotten about swimming as an activity. As a kid, I had liked it. Mum had taught me to overcome my fear when I was small. We'd gone straight to the deep end at the local baths. "Are you scared?" she had said.

"Yes," I'd said.

"What are you scared of?" she'd said.

"Sinking to the bottom."

"OK," she'd said. We had climbed into the water together.

"Try and sink," she had said. I looked at her like she was mad. "Go on, I've got you."

Of course, I couldn't. It was impossible to sink. Once I knew that, I was fine.

For obvious reasons, I hadn't swum since the toddlerbody incident, but seeing the way Lexi had cruised through the lake, I remembered that it could be a pleasure.

The atmosphere in the Tropical Dome was close and muggy. Once you were in there, it was difficult to tell the real plants from the fake. Women lay on their loungers, drinking brightly coloured juices, while the men read the paper or slept. Music blared out from the cafe shack. The wave machine came on every hour for fifteen minutes, and it was on now, so all the kids were in the water, their screams rising into the Dome's upper atmosphere. I didn't want to go in there with the inflatable alligators and the pissing children, so I waited near some thick vegetation, still wearing my T-shirt. I heard a voice above me.

"You OK, matey?"

It was the lifeguard, sitting on his high seat at the top of some scaffolding. He was about eighteen, with long dyed-blond hair, red shorts and a white vest.

"I'm fine," I called up.

"Looking a bit edgy, man."

"I'm just waiting for the waves to finish," I said.

"Yeah, good call. Good call." He climbed down from the seat. He wore a necklace strung with brown and white beads and animal teeth. "Even *I* wouldn't go in there, at the minute," he said.

"What if someone was in trouble?" I said.

He laughed. "Nice one. Yeah, I'd go in if I *had* to. But it's like *Pirates of the Caribbean*. Without the hot girls. I'm Ryan," he said.

"Daniel," I said.

He blinked slowly and held out his hand for one of those high grip handshakes. I thought back to the fist bump with Lexi: I was lost in a world of special handshakes. "Good to meet you, man," he said.

"Do you like working here?" I asked.

"You can't beat the Dome. Hot all year-round. Where else in this stupid country can you wear your shorts and vest in October?"

I thought of winter PE lessons on the rugby field, shivering and hoping I'd get hit just to numb the cold, or so I could leave the field injured. Not that the teachers would let me. *Come on, Lever. Hefty lad like you. This should be your game.*

"Listen, have you seen a girl swimming in here this week, with long black hair?" I said. "Swims like a ... she swims really well."

"Lot of girls come through here, man."

"She might have had a black eye. I don't know."

"Is she nice?"

"I guess so. Something a bit, I don't know, *different* about her."

"I'll keep a look out."

The wave machine was coming to a halt, and kids were climbing out of the water. A spiky-haired boy stood in front of us, ready to smack another lad on the head with an inflatable hammer. He raised it behind his back, and just as he was about to swing, Ryan took it out of his hands. The boy swung anyway, and looked surprised to find his weapon had vanished. He turned around, amazed. "Peace in the pool, matey," Ryan said to him, and gave him the hammer back.

I looked at the water, the lines of the tiles wavy and blue beneath.

"You should get in, man. You look tense. Water's the best thing for tension," Ryan said.

"Thanks," I said.

"Part of the service," he said.

I waited for him to walk away, and then I quickly took my T-shirt off, threw it under a palm tree and climbed into the water, trying to keep my body facing away from the crowds of juice-drinkers and bathers. I felt the tiny bubbles I had made climb up the hairs on my legs and arms. Closing my eyes, I plunged under and battered out a few strokes, hearing the noise muffled above. When I came up I was gasping for air, and I felt like all the energy had drained out of me. I wasn't in great shape.

The world looks massive when you're in water. It rises high, but you feel safe. You feel like a child again. The plants curved out over the pool, and I let myself be dragged along in the rapids, feeling the jet streams against my body. The ceiling of the Dome seemed miles away, in the same way it does when you go into a cathedral.

There weren't many people around, and the water came

up to our necks, so nobody stared at me. Everyone's hairstyle was just about the same. The wet look. By the time the rapids ejected me back into the pool, I had my breath back.

I let myself be carried by the momentum, and then I rolled beneath the surface and opened my eyes to that glassy underworld. What had Lexi said? *"Swimming is easy. You just make a wave, and ride it."* I thought about her, the rhythm of her strokes, the perfect timing of them that made her motion look so effortless. One. And. Two. And. Three. And.

I counted the rhythm in my mind. Eventually, I felt my arm coming over my head, and then the other. I felt the bowed swell of the water in front of me, and I chased it, settled into the slipstream. My body moved slowly but inevitably, as if the strokes had already happened and I was just following them. I remembered to breathe, and put my face out of the water for a moment. The noise came crashing in – the music, the shouting, the chit-chat, the clink of glasses and the rude squeeze of the inflatables – and then, mercifully, it stopped when I went back under.

This was a space I could be in. Outside of time, outside of my father's moods and my own hang-ups. There were moments when I felt my legs slowly and forcefully propelling me forwards, when I felt like she was there in the pool with me. I half opened my eyes, but the water was clear and empty. I heard the bowstring echo of voices.

For a few moments I felt completely relaxed. But then I thought of the faint colouring around her eye. Something wasn't right. I could feel it. I kept swimming, but I was panicking now, my body shuddering, the air going out of me in great bubbles. It was her hand – when she held out her fist for me to bump – there was something not right about her hand. I saw it in my mind. The long fingers, the watch with the digital seconds flickering. It was the watch. I did not have to search my memory, because the images seemed to come without my bidding. The seconds flickering. 34, 33, 32, 31. I burst through the membrane of the pool's surface and took in a huge, desperate breath. It was almost a scream. People were looking. I was standing up in the shallow end, my body on show. Ryan was frowning from his perch. *Her watch*, I thought. It was ticking backwards.

EIGHT

I went over to the palm tree to retrieve my T-shirt. The boys I had seen through the Dome's outer shell on the first day were sitting on a lounger nearby. The girls in bikinis weren't there, fortunately. "Nice pair," one of the boys said, but I ignored him. My mind was spinning with the thought of Lexi, and her watch.

I picked up my T-shirt and put it straight over my wet body. I felt the cotton becoming wet and cold in two big patches against my chest. "Give us a feel, darling," one of the boys said.

Usually, I would have said something back, maybe even flipped them the finger. But I felt so calm after being in the water. I was in a trance. As I walked past the boys, I saw my dad, and the calm dropped away. He was pale, and the odd light of the Dome made his skin look green. I could smell him before I could hear him. He smelt like petrol, and he was wearing his tracksuit and trainers. This was typical Dad: he wore his Havaianas to drive, and his trainers to the pool. "I've been looking for you everywhere, Daniel. Where've you been?"

I was sopping wet and standing next to a pool. "Swimming," I said.

"I can see that. I saw you in there. But I thought you didn't like swimming. I thought you were too..."

"Too what? Too fat?"

"I wasn't going to say that."

I stopped about a metre from him. Shot veins like lightning strikes stretched across his eyeballs. He was holding a paper cup full of coffee, and his hand was shaking.

"You weren't in the cabin this morning, when I woke up," he said.

"Really? And when did you wake up?" I said.

"I was worried about you."

"You weren't worried last night, were you? When you were kicking the TV and throwing up everywhere."

"Shush. Keep your voice down."

I could feel people sitting up on their loungers, peering over. "Why should I?" I said. "Why should I behave properly when you don't?"

I walked past him, but he stuck his arm out, caught me by the wrist. I nearly slipped on the wet tiles. My father was short and weighty like me, but he carried it better, and he was strong.

"You listen to me, lad," he said.

"Let go," I said. I could hear the boys laughing in the background. I struggled slightly, but I couldn't even move.

"Everything cool here?"

It was Ryan.

"It's fine," Dad said. "This is a family matter."

Ryan smiled and looked at me. "Daniel, how's it going, dude?"

I stared at the water, and tried to calm my breathing.

"Look," Dad said to Ryan. "This doesn't concern you, all right?"

"Actually, sir, it does concern me. I can't let you stay in the Dome while wearing outdoor footwear. It's a flip-flop zone, man. Or you can go natural, like Daniel here."

He turned to me. "Actually, Dan, you should get some flip-flops. It's verruca central in here," he said, before addressing Dad again. "But no sneaky sneakers, sir, if you don't mind."

Dad took his hand off me, and I walked out before I could see him rub the stubble on his neck. As I got to the changing rooms, I looked at the clock. I could hardly believe it. I'd been swimming for two and a half hours.

I put my trainers on and ran straight out, half expecting Dad to chase me, half disappointed when he didn't. I cycled like crazy to the lake, left the Shopper by the first stand of pines and sprinted into the woods, the patches of cooling cloth raising goose-bumps on my skin. I ran out to the clearing, and then stopped, put my hands on my thighs. I was dizzy with the exertion. I could hardly breathe, and could feel curtains of darkness closing in on my vision. I composed myself. There wasn't a sound from the lake; the instructors had taken the boats out on the water. There were no clothes on the sandy earth. "Hello!" I shouted. My voice echoed through the treetops.

Some old woman on one of the boats waved at me.

I thought I was going to have to lie down, but then I felt this great surge of energy flow through me. I don't know where it came from. It was something like happiness.

I walked back through the trees slowly, and felt that my vision was so much clearer. I could see every groove in the bark of the trees, every contour of the soil. Every fern glowing with the afternoon sunlight.

I collected my bike. As I was about to leave, I noticed a carving on the tree against which I had left the Shopper:

251293 AHC 311010

For some reason, the numbers sent a chill through my body. Suddenly, everything seemed important, so I stared at the numbers until they were lodged in my memory, and then I cycled back towards the cabin, because there was nowhere else to go.

That night, Dad brought pizza back from one of the restaurants. He had cleaned the cabin and said he was sorry. I could see from his expression, and hear from the tone of his voice, who he was sorry for, and it wasn't me. "It was good to see you swimming," he said. "You were going fast. Imagine if you pumped your arms a little bit faster."

"You don't need to pump your arms. It's about timing," I said.

"Your mother was a strong swimmer," he said.

Oh Jesus, I thought. *Here we go.*

He bucked up and shrugged. "Anyway, you looked good in the water. That's all I was saying."

Of course I looked good, I thought. *I was submerged.*

In my room I stared out of the window into the woods. I thought about the numbers on the tree. What could they mean? It wasn't the usual, *Tomo is gay* or *Daz 4 Niki*. I took Dad's mobile from the living area, and went back into my room. I dialled the local area code and then the first number. 251293.

The number you have dialled is not recognized, the woman said. I hung up, and tried the second number.

"Hello." It was an old man's voice. Sounded like there was something wrong with him.

"Hi. Who's this?"

"It's Mickey bleeding Mouse. Who's this?"

"I just wondered if Lexi was there."

"If *what* was there? Is this a wind-up? Are you the kid that pissed on my pansies?"

"No," I said. I started laughing. It was such a funny thing to say.

"Bugger off! Bloody kids."

The old man hung up, and I deduced that the digits on the tree did not relate to phone numbers.

I lay back on my bed and thought of her swimming, the absolute clarity of the sound of her hand dipping into the water. I thought of her wrist, and the time ticking backwards. 32, 31, 30, 29, 28...

TUESDAY 23 OCTOBER

NINE

When I woke the next morning, I felt ill. Except "ill" isn't the right word. I felt like someone had kicked the absolute crap out of me. Was this *love*? That was how my parents always talked about love. Like a pain, an ache, a bind. True, I'd only spoken to Lexi for a few minutes, but I felt more alive than I had done for God knows how long, and I felt battered and bruised. *Maybe that's it*, I thought. *Maybe I'm in love.*

I had woken later than I'd wanted to, but I took a little time to dress and style my hair. I thought I'd wear the T-shirt she said she liked, but it didn't smell so great, so I went for a black polo shirt instead, black being a slimming colour. I had become addicted to the hay fever nasal spray, and fired a few shots up my nose, the flowery smell taking me back, for a moment, to happier holidays, with Mum.

Dad was already up, but that wasn't a great surprise. He operated in a cycle: feel emotional, drink, kick stuff, get a hangover, apologize, become slightly righteous about health, and then, eventually, get emotional again. The "become righteous about health" stage was better than the "drink" stage, but I didn't much like any of the cycle.

"Morning, Daniel," he said. He was wearing his tennis gear. His legs were sturdy and thick. "Where are you off to?"

"I'm just going out," I said.

"Who with?"

"Oh. Just some mates I met at the pool."

"Some fellas, eh?"

"Yeah, yeah."

"Brilliant. I told you that Dome was the place to be. Is that where you're meeting?"

"Nah. We're just going to ride around a bit. On the bikes."

"Good lad. Don't forget your old dad though, eh? I've booked us the tennis court for one. Shall I meet you there?"

My heart sank, but I couldn't face an argument. I couldn't face the consequences of an argument. "OK," I said.

The thing about Lexi was, as soon as I saw her, I seemed to forget about myself. It was such a relief to think of someone else. That morning, as I neared the lake, I heard her changing direction in the water, and I felt that surge of energy again. When I got to the clearing, I could smell smoke. By the big tree, there was a steaming hump of canvas, held down by rocks. It looked like a dead body, and I stayed well away.

Lexi was standing out in the water, searching its depths with her eyes, looking for something. I made myself visible as soon as I could, so she wouldn't accuse me of peeping from behind the trees. "Hello," I said. "I'm back."

She looked up from the water, smiled, and then put a finger to her lips. She began to follow something with her gaze and then she dived beneath the surface. Several seconds passed. For a moment I thought she'd been dragged under by some beast. I thought I might have to go in and try to find her. But she surfaced, eventually, ten metres away, with a full-beam smile on her face. Her arms jerked for a second and then she held a silver fish above her head.

"No way," I said to myself.

She swam to the bank with one arm. "Good to see you again, Daniel."

"And you," I whispered.

"You don't have to be quiet any more," she said, holding up the dead fish. "I don't think he's going to hear you."

I was a little overwhelmed. "Are you a mermaid?" I said.

"Are you insane?" she said.

I laughed, snapped back into the real world.

"You look very well this morning, Daniel. Rosy-cheeked. Did you exercise yesterday?"

"I did. I went swimming. I tried to swim like you."

"And did you?"

"Not as good."

"Oh. You're being kind."

She took the canvas off the steaming mound and I flinched. But it was just grass and stones underneath, with a few cobs of corn and a couple of other fish on top. "This is my cooking pit," she said. "I thought I'd make us some breakfast."

"Won't the grass catch fire?" I said.

"No. It's just steam. It comes from the hot rocks underneath."

"Where did you learn that?"

"The Crow."

"What's the Crow?"

"They are a tribe of Native Americans."

"Jesus. Where are you from?"

"Derby. We did the Crow Indians in history class. This pit is very similar to the meat-holes they built to cook buffalo. Do you like history, Daniel?"

"My mum does. I don't get very high marks for history." I didn't get high marks for anything.

"I believe history is a circle, made by men who don't learn from their mistakes. What do you think?" she said.

"I don't know. We're doing the Second World War. It's pretty cool."

"Pretty cool, eh? All those people dying? All that aggression and pain? I'd debate that it was cool," she said. "This one is done. It's been in for ages."

She flipped one of the fish off the grass and onto a plate. I recognized the blue rim design of the plate from the Pancake House. She used a wooden skewer to get a cob of corn out of the pit, and placed a sachet of margarine beside it. "There you go, Daniel. The best breakfast at Leisure World, but don't tell the chef at Café Rouge."

"Thank you," I said. But I didn't begin to eat. I was looking at her face. At first I couldn't be sure, because of the light, but it soon became clear: the bruise by her eye had got *darker* since yesterday. It had gone from greenish yellow to violet.

Had someone hit her in *exactly* the same place? I looked down at the marks on her upper leg that I had taken for a rash; they were a deeper red now, and shining, each dash longer. She pulled the hem of her hoody down over the marks, and I looked up at her.

"Lexi, your eye has got worse, and—"

"Daniel. You have to be very careful when you talk to a girl about her appearance. You know, for the sake of politeness."

"Your watch. Why does it tick backwards?"

"It's broken," she said, piercing a fish with a carved wooden fork.

"So why are you wearing it? Anyway, when a digital watch breaks, it doesn't go bloody *backwards*."

"Daniel," she said, and paused. "It's lonely out here. I like you. You've got good mindsight, and you're a sensitive boy. But if we're going to be friends, there are certain questions you're going to have to swallow," she said.

"But—"

"Don't let your fish go cold."

She passed me one of her wooden forks and I got stuck in. The fish was delicious. Smoky and tender. I hadn't realized how hungry I was. Lexi was pushing her food around the plate, mashing up the fish. "Aren't you going to eat?" I said.

"I don't need to eat, as it happens," she said.

Oh, she's one of those *types*, I thought. Although, her legs and arms were powerful and athletic. But she picked up a big flake of fish and dropped it into her mouth.

"I eat for pleasure," she said. "And for comfort."

I smiled.

"Do you know what the bravest thing you could do as a Crow warrior was?" she said.

"Scalp someone?"

"No. It was something called a coup. You had to walk up to your enemy, touch him on the shoulder with a stick, and then run away. Now that's brave. Not a deadly weapon in sight. Sheer audacity! I can't see any of your PlayStation warriors doing *that*."

Neither could I.

"You wore an eagle feather in your hair for each coup you did. If you were injured in the attempt, you had to paint the feather red, which wasn't considered as good."

I nodded. "Well. They certainly cooked very tasty food," I said.

"Fish with corn on the cob is my favourite. My mum let me have it every year on my birthday, which might not sound like a big deal, but it is when you were born on Christmas Day."

"You were born on Christmas Day?"

"Yep. We never had turkey in our house."

"Where is your house? Are your parents here at the park?"

"Questions, questions. Let's talk about you, instead. Was that your dad getting smashed in the pancake place the other night?"

"If you don't have to answer questions, neither do I," I said.

"OK," she said. Beads of water hung from the strands of her hair and shimmered in the light. It seemed that every time I looked at her face, I noticed another little scrape or bruise.

A couple of bloody dots by her temple, a cut at the edge of her mouth.

"Yes. It was my dad," I said, suddenly desperate to talk. "My mum left in September, and since then he's been a lunatic. It's embarrassing. If he isn't drinking he's kicking something. If he isn't doing that, he's weeping over his bloody tomato plant."

"Tomato plant, eh? A love substitute."

"Yeah. And now he thinks this stupid holiday is a good idea. He thinks 'time away' is going to help. But it's not time away if we're both here, is it? I'm *his* problem and he's *mine*. So we're just moving our problems somewhere else. Somewhere with no Wi-Fi."

Lexi chewed her fish thoughtfully. "What sports are you good at?" she asked.

"I can juggle," I said.

"Not really a sport, Daniel. What sports do you *like*, then?"

"I don't like any!" I said.

"Wow. This is the *wrong* place for you, then, isn't it?"

"I know."

She smiled. "Come with me," she said.

She slipped into a denim skirt and we walked through the woods, towards one of the verges that banked a secluded cycle path. She wanted to gather some more grass for her cooking pit. It felt good just to walk with her, and it felt good to talk about the problems I was having. I had so many questions to ask her, though. I wanted to ask if she'd carved the numbers and letters on the tree, and if so, what they meant. I wanted to ask her what she was doing here, and who was looking after her. Every time I tried to ask a question she held up a finger, and I soon stopped trying.

She bent down on the bank and started pulling at the grass, tearing it up with her hands, and putting it in the pockets of her hoody and her skirt. "You can help if you like, Daniel. Don't be shy. It'll grow back. Always does."

I pulled at the grass. After a few moments, a cyclist came into view. Lexi stopped her work and waited. It was Ryan. "Hi, Ryan," I said, eager to impress Lexi with my first-name knowledge of the park staff.

"Oh hey, man," he said, slowing down a little.

"Thanks for yesterday," I said.

"What? Oh, no probs, dude. Any time. Fight the power, eh?"

"Yeah," I said, as he went past. I turned to Lexi. "That was Ryan."

She smiled, and I looked down. We went back to picking the grass.

"It's just you and your dad here, then?" she said.

"Yeah."

"Must be difficult for you. Having to be his son, and his friend, and – you know – basically his wife," she said.

I laughed. *"What?"* I said, but I kind of knew what she meant. Dad had lost contact with all his friends because of the drinking, and without Mum in the house I was sometimes the only person he spoke to all day.

"It's a shame there's no one else for him to hang around with," she said.

It's the same for me, I thought. But I didn't say it, because

I wanted to appear concerned. Besides, I had *her* to talk to, didn't I? I hoped I did.

"Hmm. Shame," she said. "If he had some adult company, it'd sure take the pressure off you."

I sneaked a look at her watch. I saw a minute change from 43 to 42. I shook my head. Then I remembered my appointment with Dad and looked at my own watch (a Swatch, with a canvas strap and two black hands). I was seriously late. "I have to go," I said.

She scrunched her hair. "So do I," she said. "But meet me back here tonight. We'll do something wild."

TEN

Dad had already left by the time I got to the tennis courts, so I walked the bike back to the cabin. I knew there'd be an argument, but part of me felt light, like the whole world was a joke. Chrissy and Tash were sitting on their front lawn, drinking tea. They said hello and I nodded, quickened my pace and then stopped.

"Excuse me," I said.

They both turned to look at me. "Yes, Daniel?"

"What are you doing tomorrow morning?" I said.

They looked at each other. "We haven't decided," said Chrissy.

Tash put her fingers on her chin and pretended to think hard. "Hmm. I know! Why don't we participate in some sort of *sporting* activity?" she said.

"Why, Tash," said Chrissy. "What a wonderful idea! However did you think of such a thing?"

They laughed.

"Would you like to play volleyball on the beach with me and my dad?" I said.

I had seen Dad play beach volleyball once, with a group of German men on the Costa del Sol. Mum and I had watched him join in. It had been a good day, and couldn't be ruined by hindsight.

"That sounds lovely. It'll be a bit cold, though. We're not going to wear those skimpy little pants, like they do in Brazil," said Tash.

"That's fine," I said.

They both laughed.

Dad was sitting on the sofa when I walked in. He wouldn't look at me. He had sucked in his lips, which meant he was disappointed. "Where were you?" I said, trying the oldest trick in the book.

"Don't give me that," he said. "I don't ask for much, do I?"

You ask for everything, I thought. But I shook my head.

"It's just a game of tennis," he said. "It's not the hardest thing in the world, you know."

"I'm sorry. We were just riding around. Me and my mates," I said. "I lost track of the time."

"You're a bad liar, Daniel. I can always tell."

He was right about that. *Did you see your mother with another man?*

"You were with a girl, weren't you?" he said.

"No," I said.

"I can read all the signs. This moody behaviour. Missing appointments with your family. Not enjoying life. All the classic signs. Trust me, I know."

"Why are you asking me if you already know?"

"Maybe this whole trip was a bad idea. You don't want to be here. Maybe we should just go home," he said.

"No," I said.

He snorted. "Yup. A girl. Well, take it from me, Daniel. Don't waste your time."

I started to walk towards my bedroom, thinking about what Lexi had said about the anger and the hate in men. About the desire.

"I don't know why you have to be so miserable all the time," I said.

"Oh well, take a look around," he said. "What's to be so happy about? You leave me here, on my own, with a tomato plant and a pair of lesbians."

I laughed. I couldn't help it. It was just a little chuckle that burst out and then stopped. I looked up. Dad was smirking too. He turned away and tried to hide it. "Tomato plant and a couple of lesbians," he whispered, shaking his head.

"That should be the title of your autobiography," I said.

He laughed.

"By the way," I said. "I've arranged a game of volleyball with Chrissy and Tash for tomorrow, on the beach."

"Really?" he said. He frowned. "OK. Might be fun, I suppose. Bit cold."

"I remember you playing when we were on holiday in Spain. You're good."

He looked out of the window, and into his past. "Yeah," he said. "I'm all right."

Dad went through to the kitchen area, and after a moment

I followed him, to get a drink of water. He was staring, perplexed, at the tomato plant. "What the bloody hell...?" he said.

I saw that the plant had changed again. The tomatoes had shrunk, their skin had tightened. Most of them were half green and half orange. *32, 31, 30*, I thought. I knew then that there were forces in the world that I would never understand. Perhaps I didn't want to understand them.

Dad and I went to the Tropical Dome. We swam separately, Dad for ten minutes before he got out and sat on the lounger with his cup of coffee. He wasn't exactly happy, but we weren't fighting. I swam deep into the main pool, and started counting again, plugging my heartbeat into the rhythm of the strokes, imagining Lexi's body folding under the water. The outside noises faded, until I could hear nothing but the rumble of my blood.

Flashes came to me of Lexi's face, the marks on her temple, the soft blending rainbow of her black eye. There were boys back at school who liked that kind of thing: girls getting roughed up. They looked at pictures on their phones. I wasn't one of those guys, and the thought of Lexi's injuries tore into me; it felt like my stomach was bleeding. I pulled myself deeper into the water, until the images went away, and I felt a brightness around my body.

When I rose up out of that suspended state, I saw that the sky beyond the Dome was dark with storm clouds and rain was hitting the glass. I peered up through the palm leaves. The green on the grey. Steam rose up from the Jacuzzis. Over on the lounger, I saw Dad reach into his bag, take out a miniature bottle of whiskey and pour a good glug into his coffee. He glanced around to make sure nobody had seen. Like a boy. I got out and put on my T-shirt.

"Easy, Dan," said Ryan. "You certainly can move in the water, buddy. Serious."

"Hi, Ryan, thanks," I said. *I've got a good teacher*, I thought, picturing Lexi's gliding strokes.

"Your dad OK, today? I see he left his trainers at home."

"Yeah," I said. "Hey, that was the girl I was talking about, by the way. When you saw me this morning."

"What?" he said.

"This morning. When you cycled past?"

"Yeah. Near the lake...?"

"Yeah. I was with Lexi. The swimmer I was talking about."

He pulled at a tangled thread of his yellow hair, and frowned. "A girl? I didn't see a girl, man," he said.

"She was right next to me," I said.

"Sure, man," he said slowly. "Whatever you say."

The frown never left his face.

ELEVEN

Dad went down to the on-site pub, the Red Lion, and I sneaked off to meet Lexi at 8 p.m. The cinder paths smelled of fresh rain, and the air was as clean as steel; the sky was a dark blue. She was waiting by a tree, her legs crossed, hair slick, her hands in her lap. I dropped the bike and walked over to her. She noticed that I was limping. "What happened?" she said.

"Nothing. I think I must have pulled a muscle while I was swimming."

"You'll want to be in shape for what we're about to do. It requires peak physical condition," she said.

"Well, that shouldn't be a problem, then," I said, patting my belly.

She took me by the arms. "You have good solid shoulders, Daniel. That's what you need. Now give me a backy."

She sat on the bike seat with her legs out to the sides, and I pushed off in the sprint position. "Where are we going?" I asked.

"Other side of the lake. We're going round in a big circle."

"Like history," I said.

The dynamo clicked, and the light flickered on the ditches and wooden fence rails. She told me to slow down when we reached a group of family residences. This was the area where big families stayed, and it was dominated by rows of tall terraced houses. It looked like one of those new housing estates, and reminded me that there was a world outside.

"Leave the bike in the bushes," Lexi whispered.

I did as I was told. "What are we doing? I'm not robbing anyone," I said.

"Wait," she said.

We crept through long grass to the fence of the first back garden. Just a normal panelled garden fence. The wood was damp from the rain, and warm from the sun that had followed the storm. The houses were on a downward slope, so you could see bits of the other gardens, and the fences like a line of dominoes. Some people had hung out their swimming towels on the washing lines.

Lexi put her foot on the ledge of one of the fence panels, and her hands on the top of the fence, her fingers flickering to avoid splinters. One of her fingernails was black, and blood rose around its edges. She put her head down and rocked.

"What are we *doing*?" I said.

"Follow me," she said. "And whatever you do, don't think."

She pulled herself up and over the fence, and I heard her running across the first garden. She was on top of the second fence before I had overcome my shock. I tried to haul myself up, but I was too heavy for a standing start. I took a few paces back and ran at the fence, jumped, grappled, and I was over. Four chairs stood in the garden, a sopping magazine on the table. I paused for a moment and then started running for the next fence, propelled by fear and joy.

It was an incredible feeling, and something I will always remember. I could feel the adrenaline roaring inside of me, and the hushed glide of the air against my skin. At first, I just concentrated on her back, and tried to forget the fact that there were people in those houses to my left. But soon I relaxed into it. My senses were heightened. I felt the wet squeaks of the long grass beneath my feet as I slipped and slid like a newborn deer. The fourth garden smelled of bins, the fifth smelled of detergent from the towels they'd forgot to take off the line. Lexi tried to sabotage me, back-heeling a tricycle into my path, and spinning another washing line so that the towels clattered into my face. She ran in absolute silence, but I could see her shoulders trembling from laughter.

Me, I wanted to holler. I wanted to howl with the rush of it all.

When I started I had been afraid that people would see us, but now I didn't care. In fact, I *wanted* them to. This was how I wanted to be seen. This was how I wanted to be known: as a silvery streak of moonlit man hurtling past the window, a moment of pure beauty in the life of these shoddy holiday homes.

It felt like everything was in high-definition. Lexi spat on a plant by the sixth fence, and I could see the bubbles of saliva on the leaf, like sap. I reached the top of the eighth fence just as she reached the top of the ninth – she was exacly where I would be in three seconds' time. She was my future. The route of gardens unravelled beyond her. I sprinted across the tenth lawn and then, *bang!* I hit a table camouflaged with a green rainsheet and flipped over the top of it, rolled across the grass. I was still laughing when I stood up. I turned to my left and saw a woman standing behind the patio door in her living area, looking absolutely dumbfounded in her tracksuit. Our eyes met for a moment, and then I was gone. *"Wooo!"* I shouted as I picked up speed again.

When I got over the last fence I saw that Lexi was already lying on her back in the long grass, her chest going up and then down in even heaves, the left side fluttering. I ran over and lay down beside her, turned onto my stomach and looked back at where we had come from.

"You made it," she said.

I could hardly breathe. "Yes," I said.

"Daniel," she said. "I think you may have found your sport."

TWELVE

We stared at the hazy crescent moon. "Looks like a fingernail,"
I said.

"I've always wanted long fingernails," she said. "But I will
never get them."

"You will."

She shook her head.

"You're a good partner," she said. "I could hear you behind
me."

I felt the back of her hand against the back of mine. It
wasn't much, but it was contact.

"I'm playing volleyball with my dad tomorrow. And the two
women next door. I arranged it," I said.

"You got him some adult company," she said. "Good for you,
Daniel."

"It'll be a bit of a comedown after this," I said.

"Well," she said.

I picked up her scent. She smelled of the lake, a scent
which is almost untraceable. It almost smells of nothing, but it

contains the freshness of life. The dark, dark greenness of the water.

"Where's your mother?" she said.

"She's staying with her sister down south. Nowhere else to go. She comes up to see me once a fortnight. I try to get Dad to come along, at least to talk to her. I'm missing the next visit because I'm here."

"What a pain," she said.

"It's got its good points," I said. I didn't look at her. Thinking about Mum and Dad immediately made me tense. I raised myself up onto my elbows.

"Do you want your parents to get back together?" she said.

"Yes."

"Do you think that's possible?"

"Maybe. I split them up, so I can probably work out a way to get them back together, right?" All the anger was flowing into me again.

"What do you mean you split them up?" she said.

"I saw my mum with another man. My dad asked me about it, and I couldn't hide it from him."

Lexi sighed. I was getting irate. I looked at her, but she was just staring at the moon.

"Are you listening?" I said. "I'm telling you I destroyed my family."

"That's not very nice, is it?" she said.

"I didn't do it on bloody purpose!" I shouted. "I didn't *want* to see Mum with the doctor. I didn't *want* Dad to question me about it. It wasn't my fault. It wasn't my fault, was it?"

Lexi turned to me. "No. No, it wasn't. Well, then. You've said it."

I looked at her. I was breathing hard, trying to stop myself crying. But she was right. And it was the first time I had ever said that it wasn't my fault. She had this way of making things plain and obvious.

I lay back in the grass. My heart was still beating fast from running across the gardens, but I felt better now. "Are your parents divorced?" I said. I didn't expect her to answer.

"No. Weird, eh? Most people in my school had divorced parents. When I was small, my best friend said to her mum, 'Lexi Cocker's family must be really poor, because her parents have to live in the same house.'"

"That's funny," I said. "What's Lexi short for?"

"Alexandria," she said.

Alexandria Cocker. I thought back to the letters carved on the tree. AHC. Her initials.

"What do the numbers mean? On the tree?" I asked, softer this time. But she shook her head. Then she put her hand through her hair, scrunched it. Her eyes widened. "I've got to go," she said.

She scrambled to her feet, and winced, holding her belly.

"Wait," I said. I grabbed her arm, but she yanked it away viciously and ran off into the trees, in the direction of the lake. "Lexi!" I called. "What's happening?"

She did not turn, and she did not reply. I swallowed hard, and looked around. The counsellor at school said I didn't like sudden goodbyes. He was right. They made me anxious. I could still feel the place on the palm of my hand where I had briefly held Lexi before she tore herself away. It was ice cold.

WEDNESDAY 24 OCTOBER

THIRTEEN

I prepared to serve the volleyball. Dad stood in front of me, near the net. He had his hands behind his back, two fingers held up on one hand. "Time out!" I called to Chrissy and Tash. They relaxed and slapped each other's hands. I walked over to Dad, who was still facing the net. "Dad," I whispered.

"Yes, Daniel."

"I don't know what those hand signals mean," I said.

"Oh right. Neither do I, to be honest," he said. "I've seen them do it on the telly, and I thought it would make Chrissy and Tash think we knew what we were doing."

We were losing by a considerable margin. "I think they might have worked out that we don't, by now," I said.

Dad laughed. "Yeah."

I went back to the baseline and served deep to Chrissy. "Mine!" she shouted, punching the ball high into the air so that it swirled in the wind.

"Set me up!" Chrissy called, moving towards the net. Tash softened her hands and set the ball just above the net. I started to move across to cover the left side of the court, but so did Dad. "Go line!" Tash called. Chrissy leapt high and smashed the ball towards the open court. Dad reversed himself almost in mid-air and got a hand to it, but it wasn't enough. He finished stretched out in the sand, growling and laughing.

The sisters whooped and high-fived. "Great play," Dad said. He was wearing a vest, despite the blustery weather, and blue-tinted swimming goggles as protection against sand. I thought he looked ridiculous, but he seemed happy enough. His arms were pink with windburn.

I, on the other hand, was struggling. I had woken with pains all over my body. My ankle was swollen, and the bedsheets had been stuck to a long, freely bleeding gash on my leg. Maybe, I thought, I'd picked up the injuries while jumping over those fences. But I had begun to suspect something more sinister.

I looked over to the lake. The trees where I had first seen Lexi were shuddering in the wind, but there was no sign of her. No smoke from the cooking pit, no red hoody, no limbs breaking the water. I thought of how quickly she had left me in the long grass, and of the sinking feeling I got when she did so. I thought of a TV programme I had seen about a flesh-eating bacteria. The man in the programme had contracted the disease after cutting himself while swimming. I didn't know who or what Lexi was, or where she was from, but I was beginning to think she was contagious.

Chrissy served the ball, but I was so angry I just slammed it into the net. "For God's sake!" I shouted, pretending I was angry with the shot.

"Language, Daniel!"

"God's not a fucking swear word, Dad," I said.

I caught Tash and Chrissy exchanging a glance. "Just leave it," Tash said to her sister. "He doesn't need your New Age nonsense."

"What harm can it do?" Chrissy said.

Tash sighed and turned to Dad. "I'm a bit bushwhacked now, to be honest. Shall we call it a draw?"

Dad laughed. "That's kind of you. But I think you two were the victors."

"Ricky, I'll buy you a commiseration coffee at the Pancake House," Tash said.

"I could do with something stronger. Maybe one of their finest..."

"Bit early for that, Ricky," Chrissy said sternly.

Dad nodded.

I stood with my hands on my thighs. The wind gained strength and then died for a moment. Three drops of blood fell on the sand, and I watched the grains absorb the liquid. A dark paste formed, then the wind picked up again and blew the stain away. The blood came from the gash on my leg, and it seemed to be getting worse.

"Looks nasty," Chrissy said.

"I fell off my bike," I lied.

Chrissy nodded. "Why don't we get out of this gale?" she said.

We walked over to the grass verge by the cycle path, where the trees provided some shelter from the wind. Chrissy had a kind face, freckles. She sat down with her legs folded beneath her. She stretched her back. Had I attempted either of those movements, I would have ended up in hospital. The way I was bleeding, there was every chance of that anyway.

"I fell off my bike yesterday, too," she said. "I was wearing shell-suit bottoms. Except they're called something else now, of course. Training pants, or something."

"Sounds like a nappy," I said.

She laughed. "Yes, it does rather, doesn't it? Anyway, I cut my knee on the gravel. Look." She showed me the little scab on her kneecap. "The amazing thing is, the shell-suit didn't even rip."

"It's hard-wearing stuff," I said.

"If there's ever a nuclear war, the only beings left will be cockroaches in shell-suits," she said.

"It'll be like Nottingham," I said.

"Now, now, Daniel."

"Sorry," I said.

"Daniel, when your father comes home, and he's had a few drinks, do you ever fight?"

"Yes. Especially when he puts Phil Collins on the stereo, full blast. Although sometimes I blame Phil Collins."

"Does it ever get physical?" she said.

"What?"

"Does your dad ever hit you?"

I put my head in my hands. I could see how she'd reached that conclusion, and I was grateful for her concern, but these counselling chats always went down the same old roads. I needed Lexi. Lexi understood. But Lexi had run off without so much as a goodbye.

"Daniel?"

"What?"

"Does he hit you?"

"No. Sometimes I wish he would."

"You don't mean that, Daniel," she said.

"Well. Maybe it'd help him get over it."

"Get over what?"

"It doesn't matter."

Chrissy was still sweating from the volleyball game. "You don't have to be afraid of talking about this, you know. When someone comes at you, it can be very intimidating."

"My problem isn't people coming at me," I said. "It's people going away."

She smiled, and then shuffled behind me. I turned my head to keep an eye on her. "Would you agree that you feel under stress, Daniel?" she said.

"Well, yeah," I said.

"There are things I can do to ease that anxiety. Reiki can get you back into balance."

Her voice, when it wasn't asking questions about domestic abuse, was soothing. And she was right about balance. I was off balance. Maybe that's why the swimming had helped.

"Are you a psychic?" I asked.

"God, no. We'd have beaten you by even more points if I was psychic. Reiki is a sort of palm healing. It's very relaxing."

She moved a little closer to me. "You can tell so much about what's inside a person from their physical aspect. My grandmother worked in a munitions factory during the war.

For the rest of her life, her middle finger was bent back, because you can carry two bombs on the middle finger, and only one on the others. "I could see the tension in you as soon as we met. Our lives are written on our bodies," she said.

I wondered what was written on *my* body. *Quarter-pounder with cheese*, probably.

"Close your eyes," Chrissy said.

Reaching from behind my head, she put her hands over my eyes. I stifled the giggles for a few moments, and then I started to let go. It was nice. It wasn't as good as the swimming, but it was still relaxing. My thoughts wandered. I thought of Lexi's back as she ran through the gardens, of her standing on the fence, her wet hair gleaming in the fingernail of moonlight.

Chrissy took her hands away, and I felt my aches and pains blossom again. "So, were you taking on my energy then, or something?" I said.

"Mmm," she said.

I turned around. Chrissy was frowning, and staring at the grass.

"Are you OK?" I said.

"What? Yes. I— Yes. I'll be fine," she said.

I stood up, because Dad and Tash were coming towards us. Chrissy stood, too. I started walking, but when I realized Chrissy wasn't following, I turned. She had her hand to her head and she was swaying.

"What's wrong?" I asked.

"Oh God, Daniel," she said. Then she collapsed.

FOURTEEN

Tash and Dad rushed over to help Chrissy, and I stood well back. She was out cold for a few moments. I could feel burning across my knuckles, and when I looked down, there were livid scrape marks on the skin. Dad ran back to the Pancake House to get some water while Tash knelt with her sister.

"I didn't do anything," I said.

"Don't worry, Daniel," Tash said calmly. "She's going to be fine."

"Has this happened to her before?" I asked. "When she does her treatments?"

"No," Tash said. "No, to be honest. It hasn't."

Chrissy had come round by the time Dad got back with the water. She sat up and drank from the bottle. She flinched when she saw me.

"What happened?" I said. "What did I do?"

"You didn't do anything," she said. She wore a dark, worried expression, but when she saw that I was looking at her, she made it into a weak smile. I knew about those fake smiles. I knew what they meant. The blood was throbbing in my leg, and I was beginning to feel weak. Weak with anger. Weak with fear.

Lexi was lying on her back in the reeds when I found her, eyes open, her face somehow submerged in the water. Her skin was pale, and her hair fanned out like a pool of black blood. When she saw me, she blinked, and rose up. "Daniel!" she said.

"You can't just do that, you know," I said.

"Do what?"

"Run away. You ran away. You didn't give me any reasons, and you didn't say goodbye."

"Danny-boy," she said. Her voice sounded frail. "I was late. I had to go."

"Late for what? I don't know anything about your life. Was your carriage going to turn into a pumpkin?"

"Daniel," she said, climbing out of the water. "You don't understand. I told you there were things about me that I couldn't tell. Trust me, I had to go. It was nothing to do with you."

"That's what they all say. But it *is* to do with me. If someone leaves me, it *is* to do with me."

"I'm here now, aren't I? God, I only— What's this really about?"

She came towards me but I backed off. "Stay away," I said.

"Why?" she asked.

"Look at me!" I said. "I'm falling apart."

I showed her my hands, my ankle, the gash down my leg. "You've given me your disease," I said.

She stared at each wound, her eyes widening. Clearly, she knew what was going on.

"What is it? What's happening to me?" I said. "A minute ago a woman passed out just from *touching* me."

"Where did you get these marks?" Lexi said. "Did you fall?"

"No! You know I didn't fall. You know what's happening. I *woke up* with these wounds, and they are getting worse, not better. Just like yours."

"Oh Jesus," she said.

"It's contagious, isn't it? It's one of those flesh-eating viruses."

"No, Daniel. It's not a virus. It's ... I can't..." She started crying, but I was so tightly wound, I didn't even care.

"Why won't anyone ever tell me what's going on?" I said.

She was crying freely now. "You have to go, Daniel. You have to stay away from me. I'm no good for you. This is all my fault."

"Shut up!" I shouted. "This time it's my turn to leave. You're nothing but trouble, anyway. I could tell people about you. I could tell them what you're doing here. That you lie, and steal."

She looked at my hands again, and then covered her face and sobbed.

I pointed at her. "So why don't *you* stay away from *me*," I said.

I sprinted off towards the Dome, trying hard to deal with the pain in my ankle, and the pain in my soul, the fury. The biggest part of me wanted to turn back, but sometimes, when you think someone's going to walk away from you, there's only one thing to do: walk away first.

FIFTEEN

In the pre-pool shower, a man was staring at my leg. I knew he was about to say something, but I gave him such a scowl that he thought better of it. The disinfectant footwash stung the cuts on my ankle.

I desperately needed clear headspace. I needed to reach that place in my mind where the world slowed down, stopped, and then disappeared. I needed to swim.

Ryan was trying to make eye contact with me, but I was afraid he would try to throw me out of the pool when he saw the gash on my leg, and besides, I didn't want to speak to anyone. The wave machine was on, but I didn't care. I waded through the lapping shallows, and then sank, glided beyond the fighting kids, the bobbing mothers with their paddling babies. I slipped beneath the bright red rubber rings and the purple rafts. I cut through the man-made current, the plumes of air billowing out of me like smoke from a ship on fire. I kept going deeper, let the air out and the water in. I let the world go dark before coming up to breathe. And I began to count. One. And. Two. And.

The world, *thank God*, fell away for a while and I was back in that gap, feeling nothing but the relentless clockwork of my limbs. I was down for a long time, and when the gap in my thoughts began to close again, I saw images of Lexi, as she had been in the reeds. I saw the things I hadn't seen when I was there. The things I had been too angry to see, and didn't want to see now: the swelling around her flickering eyelids, the coppery stain of watery blood across her cheek. I had my wounds, but she was in a far worse state than me.

Forget her, I told myself as I rose up through the layers of silence and back to the screeching surface.

I sat on the edge of one of the loungers and felt the hot, dry air against my skin. I didn't bother putting my T-shirt on because I didn't care who saw me. In my mind, I dared people to make a remark. The way I was feeling, I would have torn them to shreds.

When the group of boys who had taunted me on Friday made a move towards my lounger, I thought I was going to have to put my violent thoughts into action.

"All right, mate," the tall one said.

I didn't reply.

"I said *all right*, mate," he said again.

"What do you want?" I said.

"Steady on," he said. "We just wanted to talk to you."

"Yeah, right. Two days ago, you wanted to *feel me up*," I said.

The tall boy laughed. "That was just Thorpey. He's a queer."

"Shut up, Jack, you tosser," said a lad with a crew cut and long red shorts.

Jack laughed. "Saw you swimming, that's all. Lewis swims for the county," he said, pointing to the third boy, who folded his powerful arms. "He reckons you're quite fast."

"Yeah, well. I'm not racing anyone, if that's what this is about," I said.

"Race me?" Lewis said. "What a joke. You wouldn't get near me."

"I wouldn't want to get near you. You've got piss dribble all over your shorts."

He looked down, just for a second, which was enough to make Thorpey and Jack laugh. Lewis went for me, but the others held him back. "You fat—"

"Easy, Lewis, easy," Jack said. "It's just a bit of banter. Nothing wrong with a bit of banter. He's all right."

Jack turned to me. "What's your name, mate?" he said.

"Dan," I said.

"Nasty scrape you've got there," he said, pointing at my leg.

"It's nothing," I said.

They sat down on the other loungers, Thorpey and Lewis on one side, Jack on the other. "Was that your dad causing a riot yesterday, grabbing you, by the pool?"

"Yeah," I said.

"He's funny, mate. Your dad. The way he flipped out the other day. Crazy."

"Yeah," I said.

"Our folks are playing bingo all afternoon," Thorpey said.

"Is bingo a sport?" I said. They laughed.

"You wouldn't get them two's mums playing real sport,"

Thorpey said, pointing to Jack and Lewis. "Eighty-eight. Two fat ladies."

They laughed again.

The adrenal charge of my anger was starting to fade. Goosebumps rose from my skin, along with the smell of chlorine and sweat. This wasn't the sort of atmosphere in which I thrived. All of the school counsellors would have agreed on that. *Doesn't do well in groups. Easily intimidated.* But I was doing OK, so far. Maybe I wasn't such a freak, after all. Maybe I didn't need to hang out with people like Lexi.

"So, Dan. You like this place?" asked Jack. "Leisure World, I mean."

"Bit boring," I said.

"Yeah," he said. "It was better the other day. There was some tarts here. Nice bodies."

"The one I did was amazing," Thorpey said.

I stared at the bright blue water as Thorpey went on. "She was filthy," he said. "She'd do anything. You could do anything to her."

"Yeah, she was disgusting," said Lewis. "They all were. Proper slags. They've gone home now, though."

I had seen those girls. They had looked fairly normal to me. But what did I know about girls?

"Now they've left, this place is dull," Jack said. "I thought there was going to be loads of girls because of the school holidays, but they're all dogs."

He took out a mobile phone from the pocket of his shorts, pressed a few buttons and looked around secretively. Ryan was over the other side of the pool, kneeling in front of a little girl who had bumped her head on the edge of the water slide.

"Check this out, Dan," Jack said.

He showed me a video clip. It was pornography. I won't describe it. And I won't lie: I like to see a naked woman just as much as the next man, but this was different. Those women didn't want to be there; it was like an attack. I felt mixed up. I wondered if these lads had sisters. Mothers. Well, their mothers were at bingo.

If I saw that video now, I'd probably be sick. But I was numb then. All I could feel was the distant throb of how angry I had been with Lexi. I wanted to get back at her. "What do you think?" asked Jack. "Nasty, eh?"

"Yeah," I said. As if it was nothing. As if I saw that kind of video every day.

"That's the sort of thing that would liven up Leisure World," Jack said.

A darkness came over me. "I know where there's a girl you might like the look of," I said.

"Oh yeah?" Jack said.

"Yeah. Well. I mean, you probably wouldn't be bothered," I said, instantly regretting what I'd said.

"No, mate. I'm interested," Jack said. "We're interested, aren't we, boys?"

"Nah," I said. "She probably wouldn't be up for anything. She's not really..."

"There's nothing wrong with asking, though, is there?" Jack said. "Come on, Dan, spill the beans. Don't try and protect your ladyfriend, now. You've got to share. Mates share."

I leaned away from Jack, but the two other boys had closed in, too. They were alert, defiant. "You should introduce us," Lewis said.

I was scared and tried to justify it to myself. She had hurt me. Besides, it was just a peep. They were all talk. Nothing would happen. We'd have a quick look as she got out of the water, and then go.

"OK," I said.

As we were leaving, I saw that Ryan was back on his lifeguard's chair. He looked at me with his eyebrows raised and the corners of his mouth turned down.

SIXTEEN

They'd been complaining about the length of the walk for ten minutes. "Where you taking us, Dan?" Jack said.

"Fat camp, probably," Lewis said.

You get used to cycling at Leisure World, but we were on foot now, and it did seem to take an age. Soon, however, we passed the tree where Lexi had carved her initials and the two sets of numbers. The sun was dropping, and shadows of the branches threw us into creeping darkness. "We're getting closer," I said.

"She better be good, *Dan*," said Thorpey. "I'll want to see some skin for this kind of travel."

The atmosphere had changed. I was under suspicion. Under pressure. "I know where she gets changed," I said.

"That's more like it," Jack said.

"But I think it's best if we hide. If we go and confront her, she'll just run off."

I hushed them, and chose a stand of trees a safe distance from the clearing. Her clothes were not on the bank.

"Where is she then, this girl?" said Jack.

"She'll be here," I said. "She's always here."

We waited. After a while, they started to get restless, started to whisper to one another. Jack spat through his teeth onto the dry ground. I needed her, now.

"Clearly, she's not here," Jack said.

"Maybe if we wait a little bit longer," I said.

"I don't think so, Dan," Jack said.

"You've made her up, fat-boy," Thorpey said. "You've dragged us into this stinking forest to look at an imaginary girlfriend."

"No. Listen, I can show you she's been here. I can prove it."

I walked out from behind the trees into the clearing, looking for her footprints, for any sign of her. There was nothing. Just the dark hollow of the cooking pit, covered over with dry earth and sand. "Look," I said. "This is where she cooks her meals."

"You what?" Thorpey said.

"Are you for real?" asked Jack. "You bring us all the way out here, and the only tits we get to see are yours?"

Lewis laughed. Jack slapped at my chest. I parried his blows, but then I felt a sharp chop to the back of my calf. It was Thorpey. I went down onto my knees, and Lewis kicked me in the stomach. "Not talking about my shorts any more, are you, fatty? Where's your *banter*, now?"

I was winded by the kick, and couldn't speak.

"Let's roll this lying tub of lard into the lake," Jack said.

"He'll float," Lewis said. "We could ride him to the other side, like a dinghy."

Jack cuffed me around the head, and the three of them pushed me down the slope towards the edge of the water. I could smell the lake, the silty dirt in there. The sun was white.

"Right, grab his arms," Jack said. He moved around me. I watched his feet, but out of the corner of my eye, I saw something moving, a little ripple on the lake. Then, suddenly, a hand came out of the water, took him by the ankle and dragged him down. He gave a raucous scream.

The others jumped back. "Where did he go?" Lewis said.

Jack screamed again, as he rose back to the surface. The water splashed everywhere, and was welcome on my face.

"What's happening?" Thorpey shouted. They went towards the edge.

"Something got me!" Jack screamed. "It just—" He went under again.

"He just disappeared!" Lewis said. "Did you see that? Before he even—"

I turned to watch as Thorpey stepped cautiously towards the edge of the lake. I could hear thrashing in the water. Then Jack rose up again, pulling in huge gasps of air.

"There's something down there," Jack said, and he began to splash towards the bank. I saw Lexi behind him, her head and chest above the surface. I wondered why the other two boys didn't go after her.

Then it became clear to me. They couldn't see her. None of them could.

"Lexi," I said.

Lewis turned around and kicked me in the stomach again.

"Shut up, you," he said. I folded up with the pain. Jack got to his feet in the shallow water but then tripped over again.

"This is too messed up," Thorpey said. He started to run towards the path, and Lewis followed him. They didn't wait for Jack.

"Where are you going?" Jack called. "Help me, for God's sake!"

I looked at Lexi. She shook her head at me. I thought she was going to grab Jack again, but she didn't. He scrambled onto the bank and ran past me, shivering and moaning. "Wait up!" he called after his friends. "Don't leave me!"

After a few moments, he disappeared into the forest, and I could no longer hear the noise of his frantic breathing or his wails for help.

"Lexi," I said. "I'm sorry."

But she just shook her head again, and plunged back under the water. I saw her rise once, way out in the middle of the lake, and then she was gone. I put my fingers to the cut by my eye, and winced. I looked at my hand. There were no longer any grazes on my knuckles. I looked down at my leg. The long bloody gash had completely disappeared, and my ankle was no longer swollen. I held my ribs, in the place where Lewis had kicked me. That still hurt, but nothing stung worse than my regret.

SEVENTEEN

I stumbled back through the forest. It seemed to be getting bigger, thicker. The coming darkness was like a gas swirling through the trees, filling my lungs. I thought of Lexi's hand reaching out of the water, wrapping itself around Jack's calf and pulling him down. She had saved me. I thought of her shaking her head. The disappointment. The bruise around her eye had darkened even since the morning.

But why couldn't the boys see her? At certain points it seemed like they couldn't even see Jack.

I realized that I was limping, although I didn't have to. My ankle was healed. I missed the wounds now. They seemed somehow to have connected me to Lexi. It did not take much time to fall in love, but it took even less to ruin it. Exhaustion overwhelmed me, and I sat down by a wide beech tree.

A few metres from the tree stood five little gravestones, roughly made. "Dotty", "Jacko", "Rex", "Tigger", "Ranger". A pet cemetery. In the distance I could see the house which had once been home to some rich family, and was now an ASK restaurant. The dogs must have belonged to the people who used to live there. I stared at one of the gravestones.

RANGER
BELOVED AND FAITHFUL DOG
OF EMMA AND HENRY
12.03.24
08.09.36

My tired mind began to race back through the last few days, making connections. I thought back to eating fish with Lexi, her favourite dinner. I thought of her mother, defying festive tradition for Lexi's sake, serving fish and corn on the cob for the family Christmas dinner. Her birthday. The twenty-fifth of December. 25.12.

I thought back to the numbers carved into the pine tree. The first number. 251293.

25.12.93.

Her date of birth. It had to be. AHC. Alexandria H. Cocker.

But if that was her date of birth, I had to accept what the second number must be. 31.10.10. The last Sunday of October, two years ago.

EIGHTEEN

I walked back, past the golf driving range, and the all-weather football pitches, where the ball made a tinny squeak as it bounced high off the red sandy surface. Night had fallen, and as I neared the cabins, I saw families riding their bikes out towards the restaurants, their lights visible first, like star clusters in the tunnels of dark between the trees.

I hated Leisure World and I wanted to be home. I was scared and shaken, confused. But I knew I had work to do tomorrow. I owed Lexi, big time, and I was getting closer to understanding her mysteries, strange as they were. Maybe if I could understand her, I could help.

The cabin was busy when I got back. Dad was laughing, listening to a man with pointed sideburns tell a story. There were other people there, too, sitting around the table in the dining area.

"Hello, Daniel!" Dad said. "We were about to get our torches and come out looking for you." He was beaming. "This is Gavin, Mike and Martha." He pointed to the guests, who all waved. "And you know Tash, of course."

"Hi," I said. "None of you play bingo, do you?"

They looked puzzled. "No," they said.

"Good," I said.

"Hi, Daniel," Tash said. She was walking towards the door. "What happened to your face?"

"Oh, I got in a bit of a scrap. We were just messing around."

"You and the fellas, was it?" Dad called over.

"Yeah," I said.

"I bet the other guy's in a right state, eh?" Dad said.

I thought of Jack scrambling out of the water, his eyes wide with terror. "Yeah, he's struggling," I said.

"Good lad," Dad said. He turned back to the guests. "He's a big old thing is our Daniel. Good healthy temper on him, and all," he said.

I followed Tash out to the door. "How's Chrissy?" I asked.

"She's fine. She's just a bit tired. How are you?"

"The same."

We said our good nights and she walked next door. I went through to my bedroom. I heard Gavin open the fridge. "Another beer, Ricky?"

"No thanks, Gav. I've had enough," Dad said.

These were strange times indeed.

I opened the window in the bedroom. The darkness had a greenish, submarine tinge. I felt the surge of energy again, at once enlivening and calming. The trees looked like the thick wires of some giant machine. I could hear Chrissy and Tash talking in their garden.

"Don't be silly, Chrissy," said Tash. "He's absolutely fine. This is just more of your hippy nonsense. You've smoked too much tofu."

I sat on the bed and stroked the place on my leg where the long gash had been. I wanted it back; I wanted the connection, I wanted the trouble.

"I'm telling you, Tash," Chrissy said, her voice weak and strained. "I've never felt energy like that before. If he's not careful, something terrible is going to happen."

THURSDAY 25 OCTOBER

NINETEEN

The next morning, I cycled to the Internet cafe round the back of the Dome. I took my code and descended to a basement lined with computers. This, it seemed, was where the Leisure World rejects hung out: a goth wearing big headphones, an anxious-looking woman checking her work emails, and a boy with rhinitis playing *World of Warcraft*. These, I supposed, were my people. It was 8 a.m. Everyone else was jogging in the clean crisp air, or playing vigorous tennis while we withered under striplights and the haze of a standing heater cranked up to the max.

I turned my monitor away from the others. The search engine took me to the website of the *Derby City News*. Monday 3 November 2010. A few days after the second date Lexi had carved into the tree.

The main headline for that day was: **CITY STILL GRIPPED BY FREAK ICE STORM.** There was a picture of the freezing city centre, a statue of a boy astride a ram. The animal had icicles hanging from his mouth and his horns.

Lexi's story must have been on page two of the hard copy.

GIRL GOES MISSING FROM PARTY. I clicked the link and scanned the text: *Alexandria Helen Cocker (17), who goes by the name of "Lexi"...*

The article said she had been wearing a blue dress, with leggings underneath, and a black parka coat. She was last seen at a nightclub in town, talking to a tall man in his thirties, who wore a suit and a long grey coat. The police asked for any information, and requested that the man come forward. They said that accounts of Lexi's movements were confused due to the clocks going back for the end of British Summer Time.

A teacher from the sixth-form college said: "Lexi is a sensible, straightforward girl, and always willing to help others. Obviously we're worried because this is unusual – she's so capable, and never in any sort of trouble."

I felt my hands trembling on the mouse. I was so mixed up. The article was describing the hours before she died – I could feel it – and I was so scared for her. But on the other hand, I knew where she was. She had spoken to me. I hadn't even met her before 31 October 2010.

I typed her name into the website's search bar and read the other stories from the following weeks and months. They were shorter each time: further appeals for help from the police, a vigil organized by Lexi's friends. In December, there was a plea from her parents for her to come home. There was a picture of her father, a tall lean man with longish curly hair in a checked shirt, and her mother, her head buried in her husband's chest. The article quoted Mr Cocker: *"We just want her back for Christmas. For her birthday. We miss her so desperately. Her sister misses her. We have hope, but that's all."*

I thought of them eating Christmas lunch, fish and corn, without her. They had hope. Above the article was a picture of Lexi, in her swimming costume, her head thrown back, laughing. No scars or bruises. The caption read: ALEXANDRIA: STILL MISSING.

I kept going back to the first article, reading over the scant details of her last night out, as if the answers would somehow rise from the gaps between the lines. I thought of the man in the long grey coat, and Lexi in her blue dress. There was still so much I didn't know. Why were her wounds getting worse? Why did she run away from me that night? Where had my own injuries come from, and how could they just disappear?

I clicked on every article that had appeared in that day's newspaper. I felt like crying. I printed some of the articles and went upstairs to retrieve them. I folded the sheets of paper and slipped them inside my sock so they wouldn't fall out when I was cycling. I walked outside and tried to clear my mind, but without the water, without the rhythm of the swim-strokes, I couldn't find any peace. On the breeze, I could smell the lake.

TWENTY

When I got to the clearing, she was hiding again. *This is what I deserve*, I thought sadly. *I wouldn't be surprised if she never speaks to me again.* I felt something trickling down the back of my neck, and heard a hissing sound. It was sand. I spun away and looked up. Lexi was in the high branches of a tree, the sand leaking out of her closed fist.

"You've a nerve coming back here," she said.

"I came to say sorry," I said.

"I can't hear you," she said.

"Well, come down, then."

She shook her head. "I can't believe you brought those hick perverts here to spy on me. Like you're some idiot pimp. I should have known. It's in your nature as a male."

"I'm sorry," I said.

"Pardon?" she said.

"I'm sorry!" I called, louder this time.

"It definitely means more when you shout it," she said. She slid down the tree in a seamless series of lithe movements, but remained on the other side of the trunk so I couldn't see her.

"You let me take a beating, though," I said, trying to peer around the tree.

"You deserved one."

"You made me look like a fool in front of them."

"You *are* a fool when you're in front of them."

"But you saved me from any real damage, in the end," I said. "Didn't you?"

She paused. "Well," she said.

I thought about the newspaper articles. Lexi, without any blemishes or scars. The man in the long coat. "Can I see you?" I asked.

"Apparently you can," she said, from behind the tree. "Although it might not be for the best at the moment."

She walked out into the open. The wounds were livid. Both of her eyes were now blackened above the lids, and bruises marked her cheekbones like small dark clouds. Her hands were reddened and swollen, her left thumb bent back at a strange angle. One of her fingernails was ripped off. She wore her red hoody and denim skirt and she was shivering. "Ta-da," she said sarcastically.

I knew I had to hold back my shock, so I forced a smile. "Hi," I said.

She sniffed a little trail of blood back into her nose.

"I've brought you a present, to say sorry," I said.

I had made a headdress from a white towelling headband I bought from the tennis shop, and a magpie feather. "I made this for you, because you did a coup on me. You touched me and ran off. I couldn't find an eagle feather."

She threw her head back and laughed, like in the picture from the newspaper. "That is the absolute height of Crow fashion, Daniel. Although I did get hurt, so we may need to paint the feather red." She put it on, tucked some strands of hair behind her ears.

"There," I said. "You can be my squaw."

"I think, Daniel, that I can be your *chief.*"

"Yeah. You're probably right."

"Damn straight," she said.

She ran down to the water and studied her reflection. "Oh, it's perfect," she said. "Just perfect to lighten up my rather dull complexion."

"I went to the Internet cafe," I said.

"Really?" she said.

"To look at newspaper archives," I said.

She turned around slowly, but didn't say anything, so I continued. "You said that if we're going to be friends, you won't talk about yourself. I'm not sure that's the way friends behave."

She walked over to the tree, and sat down. She patted the ground beside her. "OK, Daniel. Questions."

TWENTY-ONE

"Are you, you know. Are you...?"

"It's best not to start off with your rudest question," she said.

The truth was, I couldn't say the word. I didn't want to, as if saying it might make it real. *Dead.* "What happened to you?" I said.

She sighed and looked up at the tree nearest the water. It had a long thick branch overhanging the lake. "I went out for my friend's seventeeth birthday party. Jade. It was the last day of October, but weirdly icy. It was getting late."

I remembered the statue of the ram on the front of the paper, the icicles. The big freeze.

"A man came into the pub. It was a basement bar. The Vaults. He was handsome, thirtyish. He seemed a bit down on his luck. He'd slipped on the pavement, he said. The whole left side of him was wet, and he had a graze down his arm. He said he'd come in to warm up. Bought me a whiskey. He was nice. Said he couldn't believe I was still at school. That old line."

"What did you say?"

"I said I was at college. I'd never had whiskey before, but I didn't tell him that."

"Where were your friends?"

She tenderly rubbed the swelling on her left hand. "Most of them had gone home. Jade, the birthday girl, was drunk. But she'd pulled my best friend, Tom. Me and Tom had a bit of an on–off thing." She smiled and closed her eyes.

"You were jealous," I said. "You left them."

"No," she said. "Well, yes, I was jealous, but I stayed. Obviously I didn't sit *next* to them while they were snogging. I stood at the bar. This guy came over in his suit, half soaked, and it was nice to have someone to talk to. Flattering actually."

"What did you talk about?" I asked. I was trying to be brave, but also trying to delay the moment when she came to the end of the story.

"We talked about change."

"Sounds profound."

"No. Change – money. He said he once dropped his wedding ring in a nightclub, and while he was looking for it, he found twenty-four quid in change on the floor by the bar. So then we had a scout around on the floor ourselves. It was funny. We found about five pounds. Filthy little coins, covered in that black stuff that ruins your shoes when you go to clubs."

I had never been to a nightclub. "So he was married?"

"No. He said she'd left him for another man. It was probably a lie. I was ready to believe it, though."

"Because of Jade and Tom?" I said.

She nodded. "Anyway, he said he'd give me a lift home. Said he was going back that way. I didn't even say goodbye to Jade on her birthday. Leave them to it, I thought."

My hands were shaking. I tried to hide them. I thought I might be sick. If she'd have stopped talking then, I'd have let her, and not asked another thing. But she didn't stop.

"As I got in his car, I felt a cold shock on the back of my neck. He must have hit me."

"Jesus. Why did he do that? What did he want?"

"What does any man want?"

I thought back to the video on Jack's mobile phone. I wanted to tell her again that not all men were like that, but I had led those boys to her, after all. I was part of the problem.

"What time was it, when you left?" I said.

"That's controversial," she said.

"Why?"

"It was the night when the clocks go back. It was one thirty in the morning when we left the bar. But when I woke up, I looked at my watch, and it was five past one."

She showed me her watch. "It's radio controlled. When the clocks go back, my watch does it automatically."

"Where did you wake up?"

"Don't know. Somewhere in the forest." Her eyes began to glaze over now. She seemed far away from me.

"*This* forest? Leisure World?"

"Yeah. Think so. He dragged me off into the thick of it, and..." She looked around her. Her breathing had quickened and I could see that she was sweating, although it could have been the water dripping from her wet hair. "Well," she said. "The rest is history. Except it's not, of course."

"What do you mean?"

She shook her head. "History's a circle. He stabs me. In the chest, here." She unzipped the hoody slightly and pointed to a place on her swimming costume. I could see a dark purple stain on the black Lycra. "And – just when my watch beeps for two o'clock – everything goes black. The next day, I wake up. It feels like a dream, like one of those dreams where you're drowning, but you're trying to get back to the surface. And then suddenly I open my eyes and I am in that lake, rising up through the water."

"I don't get it."

"Neither did I, the first time it happened. Put it this way. I live each day forward but my body goes in reverse. Tomorrow my hair will be shorter. And so – God knows – will my fingernails. All I ever wanted was long, elegant fingernails. My wounds will be less healed, more open. And this watch, which I was wearing when I first came here, will continue to tick backwards."

"When will it end?"

"Same time it always ends. On the night the clocks go back, I will wake up in the forest, with no wounds on my body, and he will pull me into the woods again. For that extra hour this watch will tick forwards. And then, again, he'll kill me."

She had said it. My mind was no place to be. I wanted out.

"How do you know that will happen?" I said. I wanted her to be wrong.

"Because it's what happened last year. It's a cycle. A loop.

These wounds have been getting worse and worse for twelve months. Just like last time. I'm trapped."

"But can't you change it? Can't you do something different when he attacks you?"

"No. That hour doesn't belong to me. I'm conscious, but I'm just watching him, and watching myself react. I can't control myself."

"Can you … *feel* what's happening?" I asked.

"God yes." She looked away. "It's like purgatory. Hell's waiting room."

"But you didn't do anything wrong," I said.

She did not reply.

"Why don't you just leave, before the clocks go back? Why don't we go now? There's holes in the fence, and we could—"

"I've tried everything. I can't leave."

"How many days do you have left?" I said. "Until it happens again?"

She looked at her watch. "Clocks go back on Saturday night. Two days," she said.

I closed my eyes tight, to stop the tears. "Aren't you scared?" I said.

"Yes," she said.

TWENTY-TWO

I would like to say that I held her. That I was a comfort. But in truth I was just as frightened as she was, and we clung to each other. "I didn't want you to be involved," she said. "When I saw the gash on your leg, I knew it was a bad sign, that you were getting dragged into the loop."

"What do you mean?"

"You were changing the future. You were choosing a different path, choosing to follow me into the woods on the night of the attack. Those wounds you had ... *he* made them."

I felt a biting chill of realization. "That's why you wanted me to go away," I said.

"Yes," she said.

"But why did my injuries disappear?" I said.

"Because we fell out. We argued. And that meant you wouldn't go after me."

I thought about what she'd said. I thought of the different paths; each decision I made taking me into an alternative future.

"But you know that I can't leave you now, don't you?"

She closed her eyes, and gave the faintest of nods. I could feel her body shaking, although it wasn't a cold day.

"You're freezing," I said.

"Yeah, that happened last time, too."

"We need to get you some more clothes." I took a deep breath and tried to raise my spirits. "Come on, let's make a night of it."

She sat behind me on the bike and hung on. I could feel the vibrations of her shivering. I tried not to think of the things that she'd told me as we headed towards the shopping centre. There was a part of me that was resigned to what was happening. If we had two days together before it happened again, then we should enjoy them. But there was another voice inside me. *You have to do something*, it said. *You can't let this happen again.*

"What's wrong?" she said.

There was that green tinge to the air again. The lights of the shopping centre blinked behind the waving branches. "Nothing," I said. "Let's go shopping."

A family cycled towards me, and I waited for them to move over. They didn't. The dad – a big macho man on his mountain bike – just kept coming straight for us. I swerved away at the last moment. "Moron!" I shouted. He slowed his bike, and looked up at a tree, but he didn't respond.

I parked the bicycle and we went into the centre, the floors shiny and squeaking, the escalators like huge metal caterpillars. The shopping centre was on three levels, all built in rings around a central core. The last of the daylight was coming through a glass roof, which looked like the roof of the dome, except that it was covered in bird muck. A helium balloon in the shape of a tiger was stuck up against the glass. I felt small within the huge curves of the mall. There were plenty of shoppers but they didn't pay any attention to us. "People can't see you," I said.

"Most people can't."

"How come I can?"

"I don't know. It takes a special sort of sensitivity. Toddlers can sometimes see me, and people who are feeling particularly sad."

"Well. It should make nicking stuff a lot easier," I said. "They can't see your clothes, can they? I'm not walking around with a hoody and a demin skirt, am I?"

"No. When I'm in contact with an object, it disappears. When I let it go, they can see it again. That's why those folk didn't get out of the way when you were cycling. They couldn't see us, or the bike."

"So I was invisible?"

"Yep. The dad thought a squirrel had called him a moron."

"Christ," I said.

We went into a sports shop. "What's the plan?" she said.

"Leave it to me," I said. The shop assistant looked at me like I was weird. I realized she thought I was talking to myself.

"Can I help you?" she said.

I adopted my dad's drunk/posh voice. "You certainly may. I'd like to try on a pair of your finest tennis shoes, please. Size eight."

"OK, take a seat," she said.

I sat down on the bench.

"What're we doing?" Lexi said.

"You'll figure it out. What clothes do you fancy?"

She looked around. "I don't know. Not my usual style. That red ski jacket looks warm, though."

"Darling, you can have whatever you like," I said grandly.

A couple of girls walked by, staring at me. "What a freak," one of them said.

Lexi tripped her, and she stumbled into a rack of tracksuit bottoms. I laughed, and then began to carefully pick my nose.

"That's not a very pleasant habit, Daniel," Lexi said.

"Yeah, well," I said. "It's for a good cause. Go and choose a coat."

Lexi walked over to the rail of jackets, keeping a close eye on me.

There were three assistants and a security guard in the shop. The first assistant came back with a couple of pairs of trainers, and began to lace them. With a practised flick of my thumb, I released the dried clot in my right nostril, and the blood began to drip on my feet and the floor.

"Oh, are you OK?" the assistant asked.

"Yeah, I guess. I feel a bit odd, actually," I said. I looked over at Lexi, who gave me a disapproving frown. The assistant asked one of her colleagues if she had any tissues. She didn't, and so they called the security guard over. He had a packet of Kleenex. While they were talking, I winked at Lexi and pulled the scab from the other nostril, releasing a second bright stream. "Whoa!" the security guard said. "That's a lot of blood. Are you all right?"

"I feel strange," I said. It was true, in many ways.

Beyond the concerned faces of the shop workers, I saw Lexi slip on the red jacket, shaking her head. I pretended to faint, and the third shop assistant came over to attend to me. It was the perfect distraction, and nobody saw the red jacket vanish. I lay down on the bench. Lexi walked past me and the group of shop assistants. "I think a nosebleed is a bit over the top, Daniel," she said.

"I'll meet you outside, by the Disney Store," I said.

"The guy's delirious," the security guard said. "He's talking about Disney."

Lexi grinned. I watched her walk out into the airy light of the shopping centre, as bright and flashy as the gold and silver watches in the shopfront beyond her.

TWENTY-THREE

I arrived at the Disney Store with a piece of tissue in each nostril. Lexi was leaning against the front of the store, the Little Mermaid and Pocahontas behind her in the window display. "Nice coat," I said out of the corner of my mouth.

"That was a little elaborate, Daniel," she said.

"Well," I said. "It worked, didn't it? Don't tell me you weren't impressed."

"*Somebody's* got his confidence back," she said.

We walked over to the drinking fountain, where Lexi bent down and wet her hair, stroking the water through the strands. When she stood up, she looked so small against the huge backdrop of white pillars, steel and glass. Despite all the cuts and bruises, that was the first time I saw how vulnerable she was.

I bought us two cups of tea from the Baskin Robbins grotto, and we dipped into a secluded corner, where nobody would see the cardboard teacup disappearing into thin air as she took it, or hear me talking to the wall. Lexi stood by the heating vents, warming up. She asked me about the nosebleeds and I told her about the Lauren Harket letter. I felt like I could finally laugh about it. I was just telling her about the toddlerbody incident when her face changed completely. She flinched, and took a quivering breath.

"What's wrong?" I said, but she wouldn't look at me. She was staring over my shoulder. "Lexi?"

She began to shiver again. I turned and followed her gaze. Through the meld of shoppers walking across my sightline, I could see a man on the other side of the mall. He had dark, neatly trimmed hair, and wore a sharp suit and a silver tie. One side of the suit was dark and shiny. Wet. He had a long coat folded over his arm. Gleaming at his neck was a bloody hole. His expression was knowing. He did not look at me. Only Lexi. A second later he had disappeared back into the crowd.

"Let's go," I said to Lexi, and took her arm. She was rigid. "Quick!"

She dropped the tea, which spread across the rubbery floor. Then she turned to the wall and vomited. "Jesus," I said. I looked back into the crowd, but I couldn't see him. "What do we do, Lexi? Talk to me."

She straightened up, but was still woozy. "We have to go," she said.

We stumbled towards the exit. I turned, and saw the man ambling casually in our direction. He didn't seem in any sort of hurry, but that didn't make me feel any better. Lexi stopped. "Come on, Lexi," I said. I put out my arm to support her, and took her weight. She began to walk again. "Good," I said.

We made it to the exit, and when I looked back, he was lost amongst the shoppers.

I made sure we were out of sight, and then put Lexi on the seat of the bike. She held on to me as we pushed off. I got up some good speed. I had to. The gravel rasped and pinged beneath the wheels, and the bike lamp shone.

As soon as we got out on the main path, I felt Lexi relax. "It's OK," she said. "He can't follow us. He can't come for me. Not yet."

"What's going on?"

"This always happens, near the end."

I stayed quiet then. The images of what he must have done to her – and what he was going to do again – kept flashing through my mind. Part of my brain was calculating his actions from the injuries on her body. I willed it to stop.

I pulled up by the Pancake House. "Where are you going?" she asked.

I remembered what she'd said about eating for pleasure and comfort. And I was hungry, too. "We need food."

I went inside and got two cheese and mushroom pancakes to take out. I watched Lexi through the big windows. She stood shivering, looking out on the lake, half of her body lit by the orange glow of the outdoor heaters next to the tables. Even standing this close, I felt nervous that something might happen to her.

Back at the clearing we ate the pancakes and sat around the fire she made. We soon cheered up, and she put the Native

American headdress back on. I washed the grease from my hands in the lake, and my foot slipped into the water. Lexi laughed. "We'll dry your sock by the fire," she said. I took off my shoe, and then the wet sock. As I turned it inside out, the folded newspaper articles fell to the ground. Lexi picked them up and I froze. "This is what you were doing at the Internet cafe, I suppose?" she said, with a smile.

She read through the first couple of articles, making various sarcastic comments. "Huh," she said. "I used to love that blue dress."

"How come you're not wearing it now?" I asked.

"That would be a bit morbid."

"So where do you get your clothes?"

"Girls' changing rooms, lost property box," she said. "I stole the swimsuit from the shop, for hygiene reasons."

"So I'm not the first person to think of nicking clothes for you, then?" I asked.

"No. But it's much more fun with you."

She stopped when she got to the more recent stories. The appeal made by her parents. She placed the article on the ground and smoothed the slightly damp paper. She looked at the photograph of her mother and father for a long time. "He's going grey," she said. "Is that possible?"

She looked again. "It's stress, I suppose," she said. "It says here they're still looking for me."

"That's from last year," I said.

"Oh," she said.

"What are they like, your parents?"

"Oh, they're great. Just great. My dad carves wooden sculptures. Animals mainly. He makes cots as well, for babies. He has a workshop at the back of the house. I used to love the smell of that place. Such a dry, good smell. Mum's a teacher. She's the breadwinner really."

"You miss them," I said.

"Bad enough to go crazy. My sister, too. She'd be sixteen, now. She's catching up. No photos of her. She'll be a beauty."

"I'm sorry," I said.

"Don't be sorry. I was lucky to have them," she said. She poked the fire with a stick. "Sometimes I get glimpses, you know. Just details of what it used to be like. When I go down in the water, I can see things at the bottom. I swear I can. On our front door, we used to have a piece of glass, with this coloured design. It was a ship. Like those ones they used to have in the Armada. Red sails, blue water. You know the kind of thing. The light used to come through it when we were playing in the hall. It looked like the ship was rising up out of the carpet."

She was smiling now, her eyes watery and red. "Sometimes I swear I can see that glass at the bottom of the lake, with the light shining through. But it's too deep – way down beneath all the reeds. Too far away. I guess I'll never get there."

I turned away from her tears. I felt my own sadness turning to anger. "I hate him," I said.

"Who?" she said.

"The bastard who did this to you."

She shrugged. "On Sunday, when it's over," she said, "I won't feel like this any more. Not for a while, anyway. It's like waiting for an operation."

"No, it isn't," I said.

"No," she said. "It isn't."

I pressed my hands into my eyes. Lexi smoothed over the photograph of her father. I heard that voice again. *You have to do something*, it said. I could hear her breathing, trying not to cry. She was getting weaker.

"I want you to do something for me," she said.

"What?" I said.

"Call your mother," she said.

"Why?"

"Because you can."

I nodded. "Can't you come home with me? Back to the cabin? You could sleep there."

"It doesn't work," she said. "I always end up back here."

"Can't I stay with you?"

"Your dad will worry about where you are," she said.

"I don't care," I said.

"You bloody well should care," she said. The photo of her own distraught father was still visible in the firelight.

"But what about the man? What if he comes here?"

"He won't. He will wait. Call her. Call your mother."

I took my sock and rolled up the leg of my tracksuit bottoms to put it on. Blood trickled down onto my foot. The gash was back. I turned away, half pleased, half scared to death, and hid the wound from Lexi.

FRIDAY 26 OCTOBER

TWENTY-FOUR

I was standing before the bathroom mirror snorting nasal spray when I saw the small hole in my side. It was just below my ribs. Although it wasn't a big wound, it felt deep. I looked at it, and wondered if it might be the one that eventually killed me. I put a plaster over it, knowing that by lunchtime, the cut might have outgrown the dressing.

"Daniel? Can I have a word?" It was Dad, shouting through.

I pulled on my T-shirt and went into the living area, thinking all of a sudden of its logical opposite: a dying area. Dad was sitting next to a skinny man with a beard who had his hands clasped at his knees, as though he was trying to pray without anyone seeing.

"Daniel, this is Mr Evans, who's the community, erm..."

The man intervened. "I'm the community welfare officer for Leisure World. You can call me Greg," he said. He held out his hand, which I shook. I recognized his tone of voice, and his I-don't-patronize-young-adults handshake from all the counsellors at school.

"Right," I said. "Community welfare. God. What *is* this place?"

He smiled. "Sport and leisure is an important part of child welfare, but we don't want to neglect the other issues," he said.

"So what's the problem here, Greg?" Dad said, doing his best to be good-natured.

"Let me explain. Do sit down, Daniel."

"I'm fine standing," I said. Nobody tells me to sit down in my own living area. Besides, I thought he might see the gash on my leg when my tracksuit bottoms rode up.

"OK. Daniel. Mr Lever. Two days ago, one of the lifeguards from the Tropical Dome reported that a boy had been seen swimming with fairly serious and uncovered wounds. A Leisure World guest had complained that there was blood in the water, which is obviously unhygienic."

I thought of Ryan, and hoped he wasn't the lifeguard in question.

"We later identified the boy as you," Mr Evans said.

"Look," said Dad. "He's a youngster. He's been hanging around with some pals here, and they've been rough-housing. It's perfectly natural behaviour for lads to get in scraps."

"Is that your version, Daniel?" Mr Evans said.

I nodded. "Rough-housing, like he said."

"You realize the importance of pool hygiene, I'm sure. But what's more important to us is that you – as our guest – are OK. Physically and mentally."

"There's nothing wrong with him mentally," Dad said.

"There are top-notch first aid facilities, and fully qualified doctors here," Mr Evans said. "There are also people like me, whom you can talk to in confidence about any injuries you've sustained. And how you sustained them. Do you understand?"

"Is that all?" Dad said.

"Mr Lever, I'd like Daniel to answer, please," said Mr Evans.

"Is that all?" I said.

"Actually, no. There's something else." He pulled a DVD out of his leather satchel. "May I?" he said, kneeling down in front of the TV.

I thought it might be some instructional film about "How to Cope with Stress", or "Ten Facts About Depression", both of which I had seen already. But as soon as I saw the black-and-white picture and the date and time in the corner, I knew I was done for. It was the security video from the shopping centre.

"After a strange encounter at Sports Soccer yesterday, a security surveillance officer brought this footage to my attention."

We watched in silence as I trotted through the mall, chatting happily away to the blank space next to me. Groups of people (I hadn't even seen at the time) looked back at me and pointed. A woman diverted her pram away from my mad ramblings.

The camera angle switched and the time jumped forward as I took my two cups of tea round the corner into the alcove. My back was to the camera and I was throwing my arms out and laughing. I saw myself turn to look across the mall, and saw the terrified look on my face. I looked at the TV, trying to pick out the man, but I couldn't see him. Suddenly, in the video, there was tea all over the floor and I was running. I put my arm out to the side, and then I disappeared from the screen.

In the living area, I could feel Evans watching me. The footage was on a loop, and after a few seconds it began again with me chattering away to nobody. Mr Evans paused the DVD, with me laughing in the centre of the screen, completely alone. It was a compelling case for insanity. I was pretty convinced myself.

It took some courage for me to turn and look at Dad. He was still staring at the screen. This was going to be bad, I thought. I'm in serious trouble. This was the sort of behaviour we'd come on holiday to avoid. I prepared to be outraged. "Get out," Dad said.

"What?" I shouted.

"Not you. Him. *Mr Evans.*"

"Pardon?" said Mr Evans.

"Very simple instruction," Dad said. "Get your scrawny arse outta my cabin."

"Mr Lever. I came here with the utmost concern for your son. It's clear that his behaviour is quite troubling, and I'm trying to—"

Dad stood up from his seat very quickly, and Mr Evans flinched. "All these bloody cameras," Dad said. "Of course you catch the lad doing something weird. Same for anyone. If I watched *you* all day, *Greg*, I think I'd find that you might be doing the odd strange thing, too. Like watching videos of young boys, and seeing what they're up to in the swimming pool."

"Now, Mr Lever—"

Dad made a faint gesture towards Mr Evans's chair, and the

man stood hastily, started making his way towards the door. "I must say, Mr Lever, I do think you'll be hearing from us again. This is not the way to treat—"

"Bugger off out of my house. I mean cabin. Or whatever the hell it is."

Mr Evans skipped out of the door a half-second before Dad slammed it. Dad put his hands on his hips, and then turned around.

"Daniel," he said.

"What?" I said.

"That kind of thing. Talking to thin air. It's not on, really."

"Oh, come on," I said.

"But I do it now and again, too. Just try and be aware," he said.

I shook my head. I was actually grateful to him. It was an unusual feeling, and it was taking some time to get used to.

"And if you want to talk to someone, you can talk to me," he said.

I snorted.

"I promise I won't listen," he said.

I stopped myself from laughing. "All right," he said, unzipping his tracksuit top. "I'm going to get changed, and then I'm off to play a bit of golf with Gavin. Do you fancy it?"

"No. I'm going to call Mum."

"I'd almost forgotten about her," Dad said. He sighed, and stared through to the kitchen area and his plant. "I don't know what's wrong with those tomatoes. It's as if they're shrinking."

I shrugged.

"Oh yeah, Daniel, I meant to say. Chrissy wants to take you out for some lunch later," Dad said. "She's going to come round about one. I said you probably wouldn't be on the golf course."

"It's like you can see the future," I said.

TWENTY-FIVE

Mum was on her lunch break. Since moving south, she'd started working again, doing temporary jobs as a paralegal secretary.

"Your dad always wanted to go to Leisure World. I saw him looking at the brochure once, but I think he was frightened that I'd beat him at tennis," Mum said on the phone. "What's it like?"

"It's like a prison camp. We're prisoners of fun."

"Prisoners of fun," Mum said, and laughed. She was always telling people how funny I was. They were usually disappointed. "There must be lots of youngsters there, in the holidays."

"The odd one or two. In fact, most of them are *very* odd."

"Oh dear," she said. "I didn't really think it'd be your type of thing, but I can't get your dad to answer my calls. Is he behaving himself?"

"Yeah, he's fine. He hasn't had a drink since we got here," I said.

I could hear him putting cans of cider in his golf bag.

"That's good," she said. "What about you? You still teetotal?"

"Yeah. I've lost a couple of pounds, I think."

"You don't need to be worrying about that," she said. "You're a beautiful boy."

I smiled. That kind of compliment from Mum used to make me wince. Not so much, now.

"Speaking of beauty," Mum said, "aren't you having a holiday romance?"

"Who told you that?" I said.

"Ah, so it's true! I was just shooting in the dark, but I've caught you out."

There was an awkward silence as we both realized that I – without meaning to – had once caught her out, too.

"So," she said. *"What's her name?"*

"I'll tell you if you don't do that voice," I said.

"I'm sorry. I'm serious. No teasing, I promise."

"Lexi. Alexandria."

"Ah, like the city," Mum said.

"What?"

"Alexandria is a city in Egypt. It was famous, in antiquity, for its lighthouse."

"Lighthouse?"

"The Alexandria Lighthouse was one of the Seven Wonders of the World, Danny. A huge beacon off the coast. Back then it was the biggest man-made structure in the world, and used these massive mirrors to guide the ships into the harbour. Or, if you were an enemy, its beam could set your vessel on fire."

"Sounds like Lexi," I said.

"Which bit?"

"All of it."

Mum laughed. "Ah, Danny. You're a hoot."

"She likes history, too."

"Does she now?"

"She thinks history is a circle which is destined to keep happening because of idiot men doing stupid things." That certainly made a lot more sense to me now. I thought of the man in the shopping centre, and of her watch ticking backwards.

"Danny, she sounds absolutely wonderful. I can't wait to meet her."

"Well, I don't really know when that will be," I said. I was close to tears, because she'd never meet Lexi. Very few people would. Mum thought I meant something else, of course.

"Oh, Danny, I know, love. Your Auntie Jen is helping me look for a place but I'm finding it difficult. Especially when your dad won't speak to me. As soon as I get somewhere to live back up there, you can come and stay with me. That's if you want to."

I sniffed up. The wound in my side was stinging. I felt dizzy. I could hear Dad hoisting his golf bag and picking up his keys. "Mum, I've got to go. Do you have a message for Dad?"

She sighed. "No," she said. "I love you, Danny."

"You too, Mum."

I put the phone down, and peeled my T-shirt away from the sticky blood seeping out of the plaster.

"I'm off then, Daniel," said Dad. "Don't forget your lunch

appointment with whatsit next door."

"That was Mum," I said.

"I know. You said."

"Did you want to speak to her? I could call back," I said.

"No. No way."

He picked up his golf shoes and opened the door.

"Dad," I said.

"What?"

"She says she misses you," I said.

He stopped in his tracks. Then he shook his head slightly and walked out, closing the door behind him.

TWENTY-SIX

Chrissy took me to one of the chain restaurants for a pizza. I watched her hands working the tongs under the lights of the salad buffet, while I got stuck into the all-you-can-eat deep crust. "All-you-can-eat" is a dangerous challenge for me. She smiled when we met back at the table.

"Your dad told me what happened," she said.

I took out a pen, began to doodle on my napkin. "What did he tell you?" I said. "It was probably a lie or an exaggeration."

"I don't think so. He was pretty calm about it. He said you found your mum with another man, and that he then forced you to confess."

I opened my mouth spontaneously to argue, but then stopped. "That's about right, actually," I said. I kept doodling, to keep myself calm.

"That must have been very difficult," Chrissy said.

"What? Ruining my family? It was easy. I didn't even have to try." I thought of Lexi, of what she'd made me say. "It wasn't my fault," I muttered.

"No. It wasn't. But it's still pretty traumatizing."

The beetroot on her plate had turned the mayonnaise pink. She didn't seem to be hungry. I was. I scoffed down a slice of meat feast and started on the pepperoni. Lexi had told me that a greater body mass helps you to float, and makes you a better swimmer.

"Did Dad put you up to this? Did he send you to talk to me?" I said.

"Yes," Chrissy said. She pushed back her greying hair, and the bracelets rattled at her bony wrist. "He thinks you might need some help."

"Why?"

"Because you're a young boy on holiday in a sports complex, and you seem desperately unhappy."

"I don't like sports," I said.

"I've seen you play volleyball, Daniel. I know you're not a sports fan."

"Hey," I said. But I laughed, which was uncomfortable. The gouge in my side was pulsing. I put my hand there. Chrissy noticed.

"Like I said before," Chrissy said. "Our lives are written on our bodies. And this is not just about your dislike for sport. There's something else going on, isn't there?"

I took my hand away from the wound. "What happened that day? When you did the treatment on me, and then passed out?" I said.

She took a breath. I could see that it was an effort even to think about it. "A lot of things happened. Occasionally when I treat a person, I get images of events that may have happened to them in their past. Sometimes I see things that might happen in the future."

I didn't like where this was going. I was beginning to feel cold. "And you got these images with me?"

"Yes," she said. She tutted. "Tash will kill me for saying this. She thinks it's nonsense and she doesn't want me to worry you..."

"Tell me what you saw," I said.

"It was so unclear," she said. I pushed my plate aside and stopped doodling. I could tell she was trying to recall what she had seen, but it was hurting her, making her weak. Her face clouded over with distress. The curls by her ear were moist with sweat.

"What's wrong, Chrissy?" I said.

"Usually it's clear what's coming from the past and what will happen in the future. But with you, it was all mixed up. I couldn't distinguish what was going to happen from what had happened already."

Jesus, I thought. *I'm in the loop.*

"Look," she said. "When a person is severely traumatized, the past, present and future can get confused. Former soldiers suddenly believe they are back in the war zone when in fact they're sitting in a pub. Because they can't make sense of what happened to them, the memories go into the wrong part of the brain, and they seem to be happening *now*. They hear all the same noises, smell all the same smells. If you can't deal with a bad experience, it just keeps happening to you over and over again."

I perked up. Maybe that was what was happening with Lexi.

Chrissy kept talking. "Perhaps you are so deeply traumatized that—"

"Yeah, yeah. Look," I said. "If you know someone who is, like, deeply traumatized. If they've had something really bad happen to them..."

"Are we talking about you here, Daniel?"

"Yeah, sure. Whatever. If they can't deal with it, and it keeps happening over and over again, how can you help them?"

"They have to talk about what traumatized them. If you can put the bad things into words, into a story, then it goes into the correct part of the brain, and gets stored away like all the other memories. It stops repeating in the senses."

"Right," I said. I thought about all the parts of Lexi's story that she had blocked out. All the bits about the attack that she had glossed over when she told me. The parts she said she couldn't remember. I picked up the pen and began doodling again.

"Daniel. I can do this with you. If we talk about what happened with your parents, we can make sense of it together."

"Me?" I said.

"Yes," she said.

"Nah," I said. I chewed some more pizza, feeling the grease seep out of the stretchy cheese. The problem with Chrissy's solution was that Lexi wasn't *imagining* the bad thing happening again, she was actually experiencing it. Her cuts and slashes were real. And so were mine.

144

"Is it cold in here?" I said.

"No, Daniel. It's boiling. Did you know you've been drawing circles for half an hour?" she said.

I looked down. She was right. Circles of all different sizes filled the folded paper napkin.

"I suppose that's got a deeper meaning," I said.

She smiled. "Tash says it means 'balls'."

I laughed. "What do *you* say?"

She took the napkin. "Well. Circles usually mean family. The need for connection and family union."

"That makes sense, I suppose," I said.

"But strangely, they can also mean that you are trapped in a dangerous relationship."

I looked up at her, and she met my gaze.

"Daniel," she said.

"What?"

"When I was doing the treatment on you, I felt the presence of another person."

"Who?" I said, feigning innocence.

"A girl. It was like she was fused to you. She was in pain, and she was taking you with her."

"No," I said. "I don't know what you're talking about."

"I felt it strongly," she said, and put her thin fingers over my hand. "It was powerful, and it was dangerous."

"You're wrong," I snapped, pulling my hand away.

She sat back. "OK. Maybe I am. God knows I've been wrong before. Tash'll tell you that. She says it's all bunkum."

I stared at the table. Then it came to me. If I could get Lexi to go through what happened on the night she died, if I could get her to search in her memory and remember exactly where he pulled her into the trees, then I could go there. I could be there to stop him when the clocks went back. It was the only hope.

I picked up the napkin. "I know what the circles mean, Chrissy."

"What?"

"Time."

"Pardon?" She looked baffled.

"Time is a circle. Yes, it's powerful. Yes, it's dangerous. But when it comes around again, you can damn well change it."

I walked out of the restaurant, already calculating my next move.

TWENTY-SEVEN

Before going on to meet Lexi, I dropped by the cabin to get some money and my swimming shorts. I crept in quietly, in case Dad was back and tried to drag me into some aggressive racket sport with his new friends. My shorts were on the radiator near the kitchen, and as I sneaked along the hall area I could see the cord of the telephone snaking around the door of Dad's bedroom. His voice came in the muffled tremors I was used to. I stood by the door and listened.

"Mmm. Yes. He's fine, Anna. No. It probably wasn't the best idea in the world, but you know Daniel. He makes the best of it. Aye."

Anna. He was talking to Mum. I decided to leave the shorts; I turned and opened the front door as quietly as I could, scared that I might break the spell.

I went to the shops near the Dome, and noticed how things had changed for me. My awareness and my vision were greater than they had ever been. I noticed, mostly, the glint of camera lenses in the cold sun, staring down from the corners of buildings. I noticed the vigilant, bullish security men who haunted every doorway, in their black shiny jackets, their breath and cigarette smoke pluming high in the frosty air. There were posters everywhere for a party called "Turn Back Time". To celebrate the extra hour when the clocks went back, there would be a bonfire and a concert in the forest, featuring tribute acts playing the greatest hits of the seventies, eighties and nineties. *Party for longer on the night that just keeps on giving.* Fancy dress was optional but encouraged. I shuddered.

In the Tropical Dome's reception, chlorinated kids with red eyes sat on holiday-style hammocks while their parents tied their shoelaces. I smiled at the receptionist, a thick-set man with a shaven head. A fitness instructor of some kind. Arms like twisted electrical cable. "Yes?" he said.

"Hello," I said in my brightest voice. "Do you happen to know if Ryan is on duty at the pool?"

"No. He doesn't come on until five. Why do you want to know?"

I thought of Mr Evans and his report of a lifeguard seeing a boy with open wounds in the water. "No reason," I said. "I just need a word with him about something."

The receptionist looked at me carefully. Something seemed to occur to him. "Hang on a minute," he said, all of a sudden smiling and kind. "Just let me check whether he's in the staffroom. Wait there."

He went over to a corkboard on the back wall. I saw a passport photograph of *me*, stuck there with a blue pin. The receptionist stared at the picture and read the little note next to it. I was gone before he had a chance to turn around and check.

Walking out to the lake I saw that there were even security cameras in the trees. I looked up at the last one, which was placed high in a tree on the threshold of the wooded area surrounding the water. I picked up a stone. I knew I shouldn't. But I gave a one-finger salute with my left hand and launched the stone with my right. For a kid who didn't do sports, it was a fair old shot, catching the lens dead centre and flipping the camera up to point at the sky.

Lexi was asleep under the red coat when I found her. She was curled up in a mound, trembling with the cold. I knelt down beside her and swept some of the damp hair from her face, which was now swollen and bright with blood and bruises. I had never expected her demise to be so colourful. I had been afraid of her wounds, but now I bent close to her, smelt the lake on her skin. I went to kiss her, but she reached out and grabbed my shoulder. The grip was weak, but enough to scare me half the way back to Derby.

"Daniel," she said.

I replied with a noise like a dying cow.

"A gentleman asks permission."

"I'm sorry."

"And he usually waits until the lady is awake."

I sat back, and watched her lift herself painfully onto her elbows.

"You scared the hell out of me," I said.

"You ain't seen nothing yet," she said.

I knew what she meant. I knew we'd got it all to come. She reached out and touched my face. Her own skin had a weak glow now, like the wax of a candle when the wick is lit. "Danny-boy, you look a little peaky. Are you OK?"

"I'm fine," I said.

"You haven't found any more cuts and bruises on yourself?"

"No, no," I lied.

She squinted at me, in the same way my mum always did. As though she could see into my fibbing soul.

"I bought you a present," I said, to change the subject.

"Another!" she said. Then she coughed – a harsh dry sound – for a few seconds. "Goodness me, Daniel. What a suitor you've become. A present per day."

I'd remembered her telling me how she longed for fingernails, and I'd found some fake ones in the chemist. I gave them to her now, and she put a hand to her chest. "Oh, you didn't! Daniel, this is the most thoughtful gift." She looked at her hand, the nails stubby and bleeding or blackened, and then she opened the packet. "What colour shall I paint them?"

I took out a pot of nail varnish. "Red," I said.

"Will you do it for me?" she said.

"With pleasure."

We carefully attached the nails to her fingers, and – with her guidance – I painted the plastic in long crimson strokes. The little fingernails only needed two strokes each.

"I'll have to stay out of the water for a while," she said. "While these set."

"Why do you have to keep going into the lake?"

"It keeps me fresh. If my hair dries out, everything goes bad. My skin starts to turn blue, my organs start to collapse. I don't know why. It's just the way it is."

"Right. That's why you ran away on the night we went fence jumping."

"Correct."

"And that's why you don't smell weird and have rigor mortis."

"Why, Daniel! Such kind words."

I smiled. "Sorry."

She spread her fingers and looked at her nails. "You are in credit, Daniel. Definitely in the black." She looked out on the lake. "It's so cold at the moment. Difficult to swim in there."

"I need to talk to you about tomorrow night," I said.

She let out a long, shaky sigh. "I'd rather not," she said. "Can't we just enjoy the time we've got left?"

"Knowing what's going to happen to you, I don't think I could *enjoy* it."

"I'm bloody freezing," she said.

I gave her my sweatshirt and she sat up, put it on and then wrapped the red coat around her shoulders. The sweatshirt was far too big, and her body seemed miniscule inside it, only the red beacons of her fingernails sticking out of the cuffs. "Did you speak to your mum?" she asked.

"Yes," I said. "And when I got back to the house, Dad had called her."

"Result!" Lexi said.

"I told Mum about you," I said quietly.

"How much detail did you go into?" Lexi said.

"Only the major things."

"What, like, *'Tall, thin, smashed-up face, dead...'?*"

"I told her you liked history."

Lexi laughed. "Yes. I *used* to like history. But now I'm starting to find it a bit repetitive."

"Well, then let's do something about it."

Lexi raised her arms in protest. "What the hell can we do about it?"

"I spoke to this woman, called Chrissy. She's some kind of psychologist or mystic or something. She reckons if you talk about a traumatic event, you can stop it repeating."

"You think I need therapy, young man?" she said. "You think *talking about it* is going to make these wounds go away?" Lexi pointed to her face.

"Well, you haven't come up with any better ideas, and I won't just accept it. I can't. Will you at least try?"

She put her hands over her face and coughed. "What do you want to know?" she said.

"Whatever you can remember," I said. But I had other motives.

TWENTY-EIGHT

She let out a long shivering breath. "I remember his car, just as I got into it."

"Do you know car makes? What kind of car was it?"

"It was a Lotus Elise 111R. Yes, I know *car makes*."

"Right. He was rich," I said.

"Maybe." She closed her eyes. "Although he had to scrape a load of coins together to pay for the drinks."

"What else do you remember about the car?"

"Not much, before he hit me."

"Think."

"In the footwell, there was—"

"What's a footwell?"

"It's the bit where you put your feet," she said.

"What was there?"

"Lots of stuff. Some rubbish. Some tools. A screwdriver. It was one of those ones with the pointy end."

"A Phillips-head screwdriver," I said.

"That's it. It was the last thing I saw before I blacked out."

"What about the seats?"

"Leather. What does it matter?"

"I'm trying to help you. You remember the feel of the leather? The smell of it?"

"Not the smell. He had one of those air fresheners. It was pine scented. Like the..."

I felt a stab of pain in my side. The gash on my leg throbbed, too.

"Like the what?" I said.

"Nothing."

"Lexi, if you don't tell me we can't—"

"I remember hearing music. He played music in the car. I was pretty much out cold, but I could still hear it. It was swing. Frank Sinatra. "Under My Skin." That kind of thing."

I could see that Lexi was struggling now. Her shoulders had dropped, and her breathing was heavy and uneven. I was in pain, too. Each word she said, each detail she remembered, seemed to open cuts on my body. But I pressed on.

"Then what happened?" I said.

"I ... I don't remember much about the end. He must have chewed gum, because his breath smells of fresh mint when I expected it to smell of whiskey. Once he hits my nose, my eyes start to water, and I can't see much. I..."

"What *can* you see?"

She had skipped the moment when (and where) she came round – the only thing I needed her to remember.

"His eyes. The blood on his lip. I try to scratch him, but..."

"What's around you?"

"There are trees," she said. I could see she was sinking deeper into the memory.

"Trees? What kind of trees?" The pain in my side deepened. I could taste blood in my mouth.

"I don't know."

"What is the ground like?"

"It is cold. Frosty."

"Can you hear the leaves crackling? Can you feel them?"

"No. There aren't any leaves."

"It was October. There would've been fallen leaves."

"There are no leaves."

"It's a pine wood."

"Yes. There was a moment when I got away. I kicked him and he fell. I ran off into the woods, but he was too quick for me."

"What could you see when you were running?" I said.

"Stop," she said. She was sweating now, her head was twitching.

"No," I said. The wound in my stomach throbbed, and so I knew I was getting closer to the truth, finding the right path. "The first time we talked, you said that he dragged you into the forest."

"Yes."

"So when you woke that first night, and the second time it happened, you weren't in the woods."

"No."

"So where were you? Where are you?" I could hardly speak now, the pain was so bad.

"I don't know," she said.

"You *do*," I said. "What can you hear?"

"I don't..."

"Rubbish. Where are you?"

She shuddered and then opened her eyes. She looked at my stomach. "Daniel, you're bleeding," she said. I looked down at my T-shirt, which was soaked, and stuck to my skin.

"It's nothing," I said.

"You're trying to find out where I wake up because you're going to try and go there," she said. "And look. It's killing you."

I turned away.

"You have to stay out of this, Daniel. I can't take responsibility for you," she said. She was well and truly out of her trance.

"You're being ridiculous," I said. "Tell me where you wake up!"

"No! I don't want you involved."

"That's so selfish, Lexi," I said.

"Selfish?"

"Yes. You have an opportunity that people never get. You've got the chance – *we've* got the chance – to go back in time and *change* things. Do you know what I'd give for that sort of opportunity? Do you know how much I would change?" I was furious now. "I'd, I'd ... I'd stop my mum from falling over. I'd make sure she never went to that doctor. I'd make my dad better... I could..."

"If you changed all that, we'd never have met."

I held my head in my hands for a moment. Lexi continued.

"Daniel, you've got your whole life in front of you to make changes. You've got the future. I've got one little hour of the past."

"I can break this loop if you tell me where you wake up. I can get you out of this."

"I don't want you involved."

"I'm already involved. Can't you see? Look at my body."

I pulled up my T-shirt. A brief smile passed across Lexi's face. I looked down. My T-shirt was still bloodied, but the gouge in my stomach was gone. The pressure in my head had lightened, and I didn't need to look at my leg. I could feel that it was healed again. "What's happening?" I said.

"*Thank God,*" she said quietly.

She had won. "Lexi," I said. "Please let me in."

"I'm sorry, Daniel. No, I'm not sorry. I appreciate what you're trying to do, but I'll never tell you. You have to go on living, and I have to do this on my own."

TWENTY-NINE

We sat for a while in silence. I had come so close to solving the mystery, but Lexi had turned me away. I was angry with her, but there was nowhere else in the world I wanted to be. Lexi had fallen asleep, and she moaned now, from beneath the red coat.

"Lexi?" I said. "What's wrong?"

She didn't answer. I shuffled over to where she lay against the tree and took a strand of her hair between my fingers. It was drying out. "We have to get you in the water," I said.

"It's too cold," she said. "Too cold for me, now."

I looked around her little campsite. There was a bowl she used for eating, and I took it to the edge of the lake and filled it with the silty water. Under the soil, the stones of her cooking pit still held some heat, and I put the bowl between a couple of the larger rocks. Soon it was warm.

"Stay still," I said.

I knelt behind her and reached out to stroke her hair. She flinched. I waited for her to relax. "Slowly," she said.

I moved towards her and she flinched again. It was no surprise that she was terrified of physical contact. Very slowly, I ran my hand through her hair and after a moment, I felt the tension leave her. I poured the water over her head, smoothed her hair back like they did in the hairdressers at home. I repeated the action until the water was gone, making sure that the ends were wet. I could see the welts on her scalp, and had to imagine what he had done to her. I thought about the screwdriver in his car. Sickening.

"Lexi," I said.

"Yes," she said.

"Can I have your permission?"

She laughed. "Granted," she said.

I kissed the top of her head.

"Thank you," she said. "I'm afraid I can't seem to get myself warm these days. I need to be in the water, but the water's too cold. Catch-22."

"I've got an idea about that," I said. "But I'll need your help."

"Well, how can I be of assistance?"

"You remember when you held on to me on the bike? I disappeared, didn't I?"

"Yes."

"Well. That's given me an idea," I said.

I looked at Lexi's watch – the unstoppable countdown of it. My own watch said quarter to five.

"Let's go for a little walk," I said. "There's someone I've been meaning to have a word with."

* * *

It was pretty dark when we got to the cycle path, but not as dark as it would be at the same time on Sunday. Auntie Jen – the aunt my mum was staying with – got depressed every year when the clocks went back. She couldn't stand the short days, and had to have a special light in her bedroom. She spent hours on the sunbed in the winter. There's nothing like a mardy, suntanned face.

Lexi was smiling sadly down at her nails and swaying on her feet. She could barely hold herself upright. "So what's the plan, young man?" she said.

"This surfer dude is going to come cycling down here any minute now," I said.

"Ah. Your best friend, Ryan."

"You've got a good memory."

"I don't meet many people."

"Anyway, he's not my best friend. He grassed me up to the authorities," I said.

Lexi pretended to look shocked. "The *authorities*, Danny-boy? You mean the *FBI*? What for?"

"Bleeding in the pool."

"Ah. That old doozy. So what do we do when Ryan the Snitch comes cycling down here?"

"You put your arms around me," I said.

"Just because I gave you permission once doesn't mean you've got a free pass to feel me up."

"It's not like that!" I said. "It's part of the plan."

We were both silent for a moment. Lexi's hair fell over her

face, and I couldn't see her expression. "Lexi?" I said.

She looked up. She was smiling. "Here he comes," she said.

Ryan's dynamo light flickered in the blue dusk as he came over the brow of the hill. He wore a thick jumper over his vest, and his dyed hair looked green and sad in the cold of the true outdoors. "Let's make sure he sees me first," I said. "And then we embrace."

"Embrace? Goodness me! You just be chivalrous, Daniel, because I'm very fragile. Keep your hands above the waistline," Lexi said.

I smiled and we walked into the middle of the path. I waited until Ryan was within ten metres of us. "Hello, Ryan," I said.

He narrowed his eyes. "Oh hey, Dan," he said. I could hear the guilt in his voice. "How's it going, man?"

"Up and down, you know," I said. Ryan slowed his bike, but kept cycling. Obviously he had good reason not to want to stop and chat. "I've been feeling a bit weird lately," I said.

"Yeah?" he said, changing gear. "I'm sure it'll pass."

Lexi threw her arms around me, pulled me close and kissed me.

"Whoa, what the—" Ryan said as he saw me vanish.

With the shock of the kiss, I hardly noticed Ryan lose control of his bike and hit the low fence, falling onto the tarmac of the cycle path. "Jesus, man!" I heard him shout. "Daniel? Where'd you go, dude? Stop screwing around. Serious."

Lexi pulled away and smiled at me, kept her hand on my arm. I gasped. "I wanted to make sure he *really* couldn't see you," she said.

It was tough to turn my attention back to the matter in hand. "Can he still hear me, like this?" I whispered.

Ryan flinched. "Dude?"

"Looks like it," Lexi said. "Can't hear *me*, though."

"Ryan," I said.

He made a groaning noise. "I've got to get out of here," he said to himself.

I continued to hold on to Lexi. "Ryan," I said.

"Y–yeah?"

"Looks like you've cut yourself, there."

He wiped some blood from his elbow. "Yeah. I'm ... I'm OK, though. Where are you?"

"I hope you're not going to swim in the pool with those cuts."

Ryan looked up suddenly, trying to see where the voice was coming from. He was staring about two feet above my head and to the left. "I'm sorry about what happened, man. Listen—"

"That wouldn't be very hygienic, would it? To swim with cuts. And I might have to basically report you to some nondy who's going to come round your house and treat you like a mental retard."

"It wasn't my fault. Listen, man, where are you? This is scary as hell."

Lexi said, "It *is* getting a bit mean, Daniel."

"I don't think so," I whispered back.

"That's because you're drunk with power. Didn't this guy help you when your dad was going crazy?" Lexi said.

"Yes, but—"

Lexi let go of me and took a step back. I felt the power drain away as I reappeared to Ryan.

"Oh. There you are, man. Thank Christ," said Ryan. "That was spinning me out. How did you do that?"

"It doesn't matter," I said.

Ryan reached down and squeezed his ankle.

"I'm sorry about your leg," I said.

"And his arm!" Lexi shouted.

"And your arm," I said.

"It's OK. That's a crazy trick you've got there. Hey, I'm sorry that I grassed you up to the management, man," Ryan said.

"Why did you do it?" I said.

"They said they had video evidence that you were a whacko, I mean – a danger to yourself and, you know, others. I knew that was rubbish, but they said they'd sack me if I lied. This job's all I've got, man. I get to live here. If I got the sack, I'd have to go home. Home's not somewhere I need to be."

I sighed. It only took a few days at Leisure World to realize that everybody had their own story to tell, and they were all just about as important as each other.

"Can you do me a favour?"

"Yeah, anything, man."

I turned around to look at Lexi and then I leaned in close to Ryan. "I need a little quiet time after hours in the pool."

Ryan nodded. "I get you. Is it a girl?"

I shrugged.

"There's this fake coconut tree by the entrance," Ryan said.

"I know it," I said.

"I'll leave a set of keys behind there, and I'll disable the alarm."

"Thank you," I said. I helped him to his feet. "And, Ryan."

"Yeah?"

"Before you leave the Dome, could you turn the heating up?" I said.

"Whatever you say, dude."

Lexi called over. "What are you whispering about, Daniel?"

I didn't reply. Ryan got back on his bike and tested his limbs.

"See you around, Ryan," I said.

"Yeah, see you, Daniel," he said. "Hey, man?" he said as he began to cycle away.

"Yes."

"Who you taking to the pool?" he said, grinning.

"My imaginary friend," I said.

He hesitated for a moment, and then seemed to decide that he'd had enough weirdness for one night. "That's cool," he said.

Lexi laughed loudly, but God knows who heard.

THIRTY

Lexi was tired, and very cold. Despite her protests, I took her down to the Pancake House with her blanket, my sweatshirt and the red coat, and I set up a makeshift bed beneath one of the outdoor heaters. We arranged to meet in the woods at ten o'clock. "Where are we going?" she asked.

"It's a surprise," I said.

"Wonderful, young man. Surprises are few and far between for me, as you can imagine." She yawned, and I could see a film of blood on her teeth.

Cycling home, I felt the bittersweet freedom of my body without the wounds. I could breathe easily, and my ankle felt loose and strong. I thought of Ryan's ankle, and how pumped up I'd felt when he came off his bike. It wasn't the kind of behaviour of which Lexi approved. I'd have to keep an eye on those tendencies.

I thought of Dad too, on the phone to Mum. His low voice. I remembered how they used to talk all night when I was a kid. How I would hear them from my bedroom upstairs. The rumble of his laughter, and the glassy tinkle of Mum's. Sometimes, if they'd hired a decent film from Blockbuster, they would come in and wake me up, and I'd sit between them and watch it. Mainly I'd just fall asleep. That was kid's stuff, but I wondered what I was missing out on now that they were living apart. Maybe there was hope.

Mostly, though, I thought of Lexi, and the moment she would wake, tomorrow night, with her watch ticking forwards again for that one hour and all the horrors it contained. We had worked out that he drove a sports car, and that he attacked her in a part of the woods that was mainly evergreen. But it wasn't enough for me to find her. It hurt me that she wouldn't reveal where she had awoken, and that she didn't think I was capable of helping her. But perhaps I would have done the same had the roles been reversed. There was a cowardly part of me, too, that was relieved.

When I arrived at the cabin, at around 7 p.m., I could hear music coming out of the window. It was Phil Collins. I shuddered, as usual, and went inside. The stereo in the living area was turned up loud, but there was nobody in there. Two wine bottles had been emptied, but there was only one glass on the table. For a moment, I panicked. My mouth went dry. Maybe the phone call I had been so pleased to hear had turned nasty when I left. Maybe Mum and Dad had argued, and Dad had hit the bottle in a big way. It looked like he'd hit *two* bottles. The cushions had been thrown off the sofa.

I went towards the bathroom. I'd imagined this moment before, the thought of finding him limp in his car, or floating in a bath of blood. I opened the door but there was no sign of him. "Take a Look at Me Now" bellowed from the stereo.

Maybe he's gone out, I thought. *Perhaps he's stumbled into the forest, drunk and dangerous.* As I walked past the bedroom door I heard a groan. "Dad!" I shouted and shouldered open the door.

The room was dimly lit by a bedside lamp. It was like a cave. But there was enough light to see that Dad was on top of Tash, and in the twist of sheets I could see her legs behind his back. I couldn't move. To be fair to Tash, she tried to push him away when she saw me. "Ricky," she hissed. "It's Daniel."

But Dad didn't move. He didn't turn around, either. He just waited there, the muscles in his shoulders shaking slightly with his own weight. The other glass of wine was half empty on the bedside table.

"D-Daniel, I—" Tash stuttered as she pulled a pillow over her chest.

"I don't want to hear it," I said to her.

"Daniel, you shouldn't speak to Tash like that," Dad said solemnly, still not turning around.

"You can piss off," I said. "I thought you were sorting yourself out, but you're just weak. You're a ... you're a typical man."

I stormed down the hall. I heard movement from the bedroom, and soon Dad was out in one of the ridiculous towelling robes. "You come back here, lad," he said.

I turned to face him. "What?"

"A typical man?" he said. "What's that supposed to mean?"

"What do *you* think?" I said, pointing to the bedroom.

"Tash and I are free, consenting adults."

"You're drunk adults," I said.

"We've had a couple of … hang on. I don't have to explain myself to you, Daniel. I can do what I like."

"And you do," I said. "Five minutes ago you were telling me women were sent from the devil."

"I never said that. Per se. They're not."

"I know! I know they're not! I came back here this afternoon, and you were talking to Mum."

His face changed. He blinked a couple of times, and his shoulders dropped, but he didn't say anything.

"Do you know how that made me feel?" I said. "I was … happy. I thought you might…"

He laughed. "You thought we might *what*? Get back together? Are you mad?"

That hurt. It hurt because in my heart I knew they wouldn't get back together and I had *always* known that they wouldn't. It's painful to see your illusions of hope for what they really are. Painful and maddening. "You stink of booze," I hissed. "This whole place reeks."

"Bloody hell. Sometimes you talk to me like you're *my* father."

"Sometimes it bloody feels like it," I said.

He stopped for a moment, as though my remark had sobered him up a little. But then he went back on the attack.

Down the same old obvious roads. "I notice you never reacted this way when you caught your mother playing away from home. And *she* was married. I'm perfectly free to do whatever I—"

"Stop blaming me!" I screamed. "Stop blaming me for that. I didn't do anything wrong." I got right up in his face now, and I noticed that he backed off a step. "Do you really think I wanted to see them together? Do you really think I was happy about it? I didn't want to split you up from Mum. You *forced* me to tell you. Think about how that feels. Think about somebody else for a bloody change."

I grabbed my shorts from the radiator, and a couple of jumpers. I turned, ran out of the cabin door, picked up my bike and cycled away. A few hundred yards down the path, I turned to look back, still furious, and I thought I saw the flash of a red coat moving towards our cabin. I blinked, and it was gone. I wondered, again, if I was finally losing it.

THIRTY-ONE

The forest felt calm to me. Maybe it was the release of having shouted at Dad, or maybe it was the time of year: the bluster of autumn almost over, a final intake of breath before the long descent into winter. I was here for two more nights, and while I didn't know exactly what the next forty-eight hours held, I knew it wouldn't be calm.

The lamp of my bicycle spread that submarine green light across the trees, which seemed to part for me. I could feel the dark wake of my path falling heavily behind.

Lexi was late. I sat down and waited, staring out on the black lake. After a while, I noticed something red floating on the water over to my right. Her coat. I feared the worst, and ran out towards the edge of the lake. I was about to wade out into the water when I heard her voice.

"Hello, Daniel," she said.

It was as if she had appeared from nowhere. She was a few metres away, kneeling before the lake, cupping her hands to wet her hair. She was shivering.

"Where have you been? Where did you *come* from?" I said. I pointed out to the coat. "I thought something terrible had happened. I thought you were—"

"I'm fine," she said. "Just a bit cold, that's all."

"That's hardly surprising, is it? How did your coat get out there?"

She shrugged.

"You must be freezing," I said, wrapping one of the jumpers I had brought around her shoulders.

"Why, thank you, Daniel," she said. "Will you bring my blanket?"

"Oh, you don't need that. I've got more warm clothes."

"I'm getting rid of it," she said. I retrieved the blanket from where it lay beneath the outdoor heater. Lexi took it from me, folded it and tossed it into the lake.

"What did you do that for?"

"I think it's a good idea to do a spring clean each time I go. That blanket was covered in blood and all sorts. Not very hygienic."

"But what about tonight and tomorrow?" I said.

She looked at the ground. "When I go tonight, that's it. The next time I wake up, I'll be… Well, it'll be one o'clock, and he'll be there."

I put my hands on my head. "So that's the end? Can I see you on Sunday before I go? When do you wake up again?"

"Sunday night."

"Sunday night? I'll be gone!"

"I'm sorry."

I kicked at the sand and walked away a few paces. "This is a disaster," I said. "Why didn't you tell me before?"

Lexi stood up slowly. "Forgive me if I can't raise too much sympathy for you, Daniel. I'd rather it wasn't like this, myself."

I stopped. "You're right. I'm sorry."

"Well. We should make the most of the rest of it," she said. "Or we can always spend our last night together with you moping around like a two-year-old who's had his dummy nabbed."

I looked out on the lake. "Yeah. I've had a bit of a bad night so far, that's all."

"What happened?" Lexi said.

"I caught my Dad in bed with the woman next door."

"Your mystic?"

"No. The mystic's sister. Just when I thought there was some hope, he goes and gets drunk and does something stupid."

"Stupid?"

"Yes."

"But it's not stupid. By the sounds of it, a couple of weeks ago he couldn't have even *talked* to a woman without getting his face slapped."

"What do you mean?"

"Well, you've built him up. You got him to play volleyball with the neighbours, you got him to meet people..."

"Are you blaming me?" I said.

"Not blaming. I'm giving you the credit. You're making him better."

"I don't get it."

"He's behaving more like a normal person again."

"He's still drinking," I said.

"One step at a time," she said.

She reached out and scratched the back of my hand gently with her long fake nails. She was so cold. "It's about time you cheered up, Daniel," she said.

I managed a watery smile. "Let's go," I said.

I cycled slowly, to lessen the wind-chill. Lexi lay her head on my shoulder. It was the weight of a bird. We passed the all-weather pitches, and the tennis courts, and the climbing wall, and the assault course. Workmen were setting up the stage for the Turn Back Time festival. Eventually, the Dome rose on the horizon, like the cool blue heart of the forest.

I left the bicycle outside and retrieved the key from behind the fake coconut tree.

"You didn't!" Lexi said, as she had said before. But her voice was reedy and weak now. "This time you've outdone yourself."

We walked through the darkened reception and into the changing rooms. I switched on the light and took off my T-shirt without even thinking.

"You're the model of body confidence these days, aren't you?" Lexi said.

I smiled. "Your turn," I said.

"Not on your life," she said, and went into the toilet cubicle to change.

* * *

We walked through the disinfectant pool and emerged into the empty Dome. The lights were dimmed, and came mostly from under the water. The elevator music had been turned off, the food and drink stalls were closed, and the only sound was that of the waterfalls and rapids. The real palms and the fake trees dripped with condensation.

"What do you think? You need to swim, but you need to keep warm, too. So I thought this was a nice compromise."

"It's beautiful," she said.

"Well. It's not *beautiful*. It's a bit fake."

"Fake can be beautiful. Like these fingernails," she said. "I absolutely love it here, Daniel. How did you get the keys?"

"My best friend Ryan gave them to me," I said.

She laughed. We walked around to the deep end of the pool. The blue tiles shimmered on the pool floor, and the lights glowed softly on the walls beneath the water. Steam rose up into our faces. Lexi took my hand and we fell forward into the silence and brilliance of the water.

We went deeper and deeper. I opened my eyes, and beyond the white fuzz of bubbles I was making, I could see Lexi, one arm out in front of her, long and still. In spite of the injuries and weakness, in the water, all of her grace and beauty remained intact.

She took hold of my hand and pulled me down. For a moment I thought she might never let me rise, but then I decided that I didn't care. There were worse ways to go. Eventually, as I was running out of air, she wrapped her body around mine and we arced upwards together, twining our limbs as we burst through the surface and into the muggy air. I was dizzy with the lack of oxygen. It felt good.

"I can hardly ... breathe," I said.

"But you can certainly swim," she said.

She arrowed back under and headed for the rapids. I followed her, and caught the tail of her slipstream, which pulled me along. I began to move my arms and legs to her perfect rhythm. Soon I could feel my heart tune in to the beat of her strokes. And then I was back in that silent space, my body weightless and free. I closed my eyes and imagined the blackish green water of the lake, with the slinky bodies of the reeds dancing around me. I pictured the dull metal grey of the fish down there, the grainy silt like TV static, and Lexi up ahead. She pointed down and I could see something glinting red. It was the glass in the door of her old home: the red galleon riding the bright blue waves. The colours reflected on her face.

I opened my eyes and woke from the vision. I surfaced and the moving water of the rapids carried me through a dark tunnel of thick vegetation, which cast a strange green light. Lexi was behind me, holding on.

"Hello," she said.

"Hi," I said.

"I feel much better."

"Good. You look better."

"You're lying, but thank you," she said. She was right. The water had diluted the blood, which ran across her face in rusty streaks. "Do you mind? About these wounds? Do they make me look horrible?"

"No," I said. I thought of the picture of her face in the newspaper, before she died. Her fleshy cheeks and her head thrown back. Her eyes were still shining, but that was about it.

"But you don't just like me because I'm battered and bruised? You're not some kind of weirdo?"

"No. I can see past the scars, that's all."

She nodded and we kissed as the current dragged us through the dark tunnel of green light. "I'm going to miss you," she said.

I realized then that it was *me* who would leave. On Sunday morning I would go home to our house. I would live with my dad, and eventually see my mum. I would go back to my average school, my average life, while Lexi was stuck here in this murderous loop.

Lexi seemed to read what I was thinking. "It's OK," she said. She smiled. I didn't know if the smile was fake, but it was certainly beautiful.

When we got out of the pool, Lexi's temperature began to drop rapidly. We were by the shell of the Dome. I looked over Lexi's shoulder, but the night outside was so dark and misty that I could only see our reflections in the plastic glass. Then my eyes refocused and I saw him. The man. He was wearing his half-soaked coat now and smiling. The wound in his neck was spilling purple blood. Lexi had her back to him, and I tried to keep my expression neutral.

"What's wrong?" she said.

"Nothing," I said. "But you're freezing. I've got an idea.

Come on, let's go."

I dragged her away from the shell and down the side of the pool. Past the food shack there was an adults-only area with a hot steam room. The door was made from frosted glass, and inside, beyond the heavy eucalyptus steam clouds, there was a tiled bench to sit on. "Perfect," Lexi said, resting in the corner.

I closed the door and sat beside her, the heat opening my pores. I could feel the sweat running down my chest. Lexi stroked back her hair. She was veiled in steam beside me.

"This is a treat," she said. Her voice echoed in the chamber of blue and white tiles.

"Down in the water," I said. "I felt like I was having a vision. Does that sound stupid?"

"No. What did you see?"

"I saw your front door. With the Armada ship. It was like we were in the lake."

"You have excellent mindsight," Lexi said.

I laughed.

"You know, the Crow used to send young men your age out into remote places, so they could have visions," she said.

"Just the boys?"

"Yes. They wanted the males to get in touch with the spiritual world."

"They didn't think the women were capable?" I said.

Lexi laughed. "They believed women were *already* in touch with the spirit world, because they could give birth to children."

Sometimes, when Lexi talked, I could feel the life she would never have unravelling.

"Anyway," she said. "The boy would go out into the wilderness, without food and water, and wait for his spirit guide to come and tell him words of wisdom, or even tell him about the future."

"Are you my spirit guide?" I asked.

She laughed again. "I'm not the person to ask about the future," she said.

"But you are," I said. "You know what's going to happen tomorrow night."

"Stop it, Daniel."

"I don't see the harm in telling me where you're going to be. I could help you. I could do something."

"He's too strong. I thought about telling you, but when I saw that stab wound in your stomach, I knew he was too strong."

"You don't know how strong I am," I said. "You've no idea. I can match him."

"I don't want you to match him. I don't want you to be anything like him. It's not brave to be like him. All that physical nonsense. It takes guts to be gentle, Daniel. That's what you've got."

I turned on her. "I don't *need* to know where you wake up. I can just go and find him. I can do it now, or tomorrow. He was out there, a minute ago. I saw him. He can't have got far," I said. I stood up, but she pulled gently on my arm.

"Sit down," she said.

"I can find him, and I can smash him."

"Smash him?"

"I'll confront him. I'll get Ryan to help."

"It won't do any good," she said.

I stopped talking. The knowledge was filling my mind. The wound in his neck. The fact that I couldn't see him on Evans's security DVD. I knew what she was going to say.

"He's dead," she said.

"But. In the newspaper. Witnesses said they saw you together. He bought you a drink. The barman must have seen him."

"He was alive then."

"I don't understand."

"I killed him."

I was reeling from the heat of the steam, but the air in my lungs felt cool and sharp. "What happened?" I said.

"He thought I was gone. He was just lying there on top of me. I'd picked up the screwdriver from the car and put it in my pocket, but I hadn't been able to reach it while he was attacking me."

"Why?"

"He had a knife to my throat. But he thought I was dead. He relaxed. I could feel the blood coming up into my mouth and I knew I hadn't got long. I grabbed the screwdriver and jammed it into his neck."

In the gaps between the clouds of steam that rolled out of the vent in the floor, I stared at her, and realized that the new dark blood on her cheeks didn't belong to her.

"Why didn't you tell me?" I said.

"Tell you what? That I'm a murderer?"

"Lexi, you're not a..." Even in the clouded room I could feel that she'd turned away, that she was ashamed. "Can't you stop yourself from killing him?" I asked.

"No. I've told you. I'm just watching it all happen," she said. "I'm feeling it and watching it, but I can't do anything. I'm witnessing my sin. I deserve this."

"No," I said. "That's not true." I said those words she had once said to me. "Lexi, it wasn't your fault."

She didn't reply. Through the vapour I could see that the scars on her legs were like pink icicles; deep grazes sparkled with tiny red grains, and I saw a new slash drawn across her arm like a jet stream. Pine needles fell from her hair. She put her head back against the tiles and sighed.

"Isn't it possible that we could just stay awake? If we stay awake then he can't take you," I said.

"It doesn't work like that."

"But we could try."

"Do me a favour, young man," she said.

"Yes," I said.

"Remember this week," she said.

"How could I ever forget it?" I said.

"Just keep playing it in your head. Remember the things we've said and done. It's the only way I can exist in the real world. Remember this week and play it on a loop."

"I will," I said. "I promise."

She extended her fist towards me, and I touched it with mine, felt the knuckles slip into the grooves again.

In the heat, I could feel the badness sweating out of my body and turning to vapour. I felt pure and clean. I reached out to her through the steam, but my hand touched only the tiles. She was gone.

SATURDAY 27 OCTOBER

THIRTY-TWO

The next morning, I didn't want to know. I lay in bed for hours, awake. I could hear Dad in the kitchen, doing the deep breathing that meant he had a hangover. Gavin came in and wound him up about Tash. Dad laughed and made coffee, and then they went out.

It was noon before I could bring myself to open the Aztec-patterned curtains and look out on a world without Lexi. The day was dry and crisp, a dusting of frost on the cabins, but only in the shade. Where was she, now? Where did she go?

I thought about school. I was due to return next week. After their holidays, I often heard my classmates talking about holiday romances. Most of them were liars: lads with self-inflicted love bites on their shoulders, telling tall tales about having wild sex with women in their thirties who seemed to share a lot of physical characteristics with our Geography teacher. The ones who had really been in love on holiday didn't talk about it much. They just came back acting differently. After her family trip to Newquay, Ellie Marsh returned with a double-pierced ear; she'd started wearing Vans, and had dyed her hair with lemon juice. With Jack Sansom, it was brogues and the New York Dolls.

What would I have? I didn't know what music Lexi liked, and most of her clothes she had stolen from the women's changing rooms. And she was dead, for God's sake. Chances were, I'd be going back to school even weirder than I was before I left. I thought of the red glint of her front door. I still had so many questions.

In the kitchen, the wine bottles had been thrown away, and the glasses cleaned. The bedsheets were in the washing machine. Tash's make-up compact was on the worktop, some of the powder – the colour of her skin – was dashed on the Formica.

I put my hand behind the tiny green buds that just a week ago had been ripe tomatoes.

My swimming shorts were still wet, but I put them in my bag anyway. Maybe if I swam, if I found the old rhythm, the visions would come. I might see her, and in my visions she might tell me where she woke. I doubted it, but there was nothing else to do.

I went outside, where I could hear Tash and Chrissy arguing in the living area of their cabin.

"How could you?" Chrissy said.

"Very easily, after two bottles of wine," Tash said.

"He's so vulnerable, Tash."

"I wish you'd stop going on about that boy. He's just a teenager. He'll be fine."

"I wasn't talking about the boy. The boy is perfectly strong. I was talking about his father."

Well, I thought, *that's a little victory*. The sisters began arguing about breakfast. Tash wanted a bacon sandwich, but there was only pumpernickel bread. They could have been arguing about a world war and I would have thought it was pointless. I cared only about Lexi.

I cycled over to the Dome, but I felt the strength draining out of me as soon as I got there. The memories of the previous night dragged me down. My head was in a bad way.

The wave machine was on when I got to the pool, and it was full of little scallies. I didn't care. I waded on in through the rubber rings and the inflatable dinosaurs, and the kick-floats and buoys. When I tried to swim, the chlorine stung my eyes. When I closed them, the man's face emerged in my mind. I could find no rhythm; I could barely stay afloat. I sucked in breaths at the surface, which was covered in a scum of spit and kid pee.

"Hey, Dan!"

It was Ryan, by the side of the pool. I swam slowly over to him. He crouched down and looked around him. "How did it go?" he said.

"It's not a night I'll forget in a hurry," I said.

"Nice one. Hey, are you coming to Turn Back Time tonight? Me and the fellas are going as Teen Wolfs. We're going to Fancy Stan's Dress Shop this afternoon to pick up the costumes. Keeping it eighties. A whole extra hour to party!"

"I don't know if I'll make it. I feel a bit strange, to be

honest," I said. I planned to scour the forest for Lexi, although I knew it was hopeless.

"You're not going to disappear again, are you?" Ryan said.

"No," I said.

"Hey listen, man. I wanted to give you the heads-up about something," Ryan said. He lowered his voice and looked around again. "Do you know the guy Evans, from welfare services?"

"Yeah. Last time I saw him, my dad was dragging his arse out into the forest," I said.

Ryan laughed. "I'd have paid good money to see that. Anyway, he's been in here, asking questions about you."

"What kind of questions?"

"If we've seen you, who you were with, what you were doing. Asking if we've spotted you acting strangely or aggressively."

"What did you say?"

"I said I hadn't seen you. Which is nearly true, seeing as how you vanished into thin air last time."

I glanced across the pool. There seemed to be a greater security presence than usual. "I'd better make myself scarce," I said.

Ryan bent down. "They said you smashed up a security camera," he said.

"Well," I said.

"Good for you, man. Fight for civil liberties. Hopefully see you tonight."

"Thanks, Ryan," I said.

I swam to the shallow end and stepped out of the pool.

One of the security men lifted the lapel of his jacket and spoke into it as I walked to the changing rooms. I got dressed quickly and made my way through the reception area and out past the coconut tree. As I unlocked my bike, I heard a familiar noise, getting louder. There were so few cars at Leisure World, it took me a while to recognize the sound of a Ford Focus revved to the max in second gear. *Dad.* The car flew past, his pale face turned towards the entrance of the Dome. I heard him slam on the brakes. A second later he reversed and buzzed down the window.

"Daniel! Get in! Leave that bike there. Come on, chop-chop," he said.

People were staring at him, frowning and chattering.

"What's going on?" I said.

"There's no time, lad. Get in and I'll tell you."

I looked behind me, and through the doors to the Dome, I could see a security guard approaching. I jogged over to the car and got in.

Dad put his foot down. "Are you even sober enough to drive?" I asked.

"Never mind about that. I'm doing my best for us."

"What happened?"

"That tosser from the 'Community of Child Welfare Dickheads' came round to the cabin."

"Evans?"

"That's the one. He comes in with another of his DVDs, and low and behold it's you chucking rocks at a camera."

I rolled my eyes. "I'll pay for it out of my pocket money," I said.

"That's not the problem," Dad said as we overtook a family of cyclists. "He's got some official order for you to be placed in a secure unit on site until the police and social services arrive."

"What?" I said.

"He reckons he's got enough evidence to get you temporarily taken away."

"What did you say?"

"Probably best if I don't repeat that, all things considered."

"Jesus," I said. "This place."

I looked at the cabins falling away as we drove out beyond the residential section and into the forest. "Dad?" I said.

"Aye."

"The cabin is back there."

"I know."

"So where are we going?"

"We're off, Daniel. The bags are in the boot. We can't be hanging around here. We need to get home so I can speak to a lawyer."

"We're leaving Leisure World?"

"Good riddance to the place," he said.

I looked at him. He wore that expression of determination he sometimes had when he was fixed on doing something stupid. I felt my stomach knotting. Maybe I couldn't do anything about Lexi, maybe I'd seen her for the last time, but I wasn't ready to leave. I couldn't quit now.

"Look," Dad said. "It was a mistake to bring you here in the first place. I admit it. The place is a hellhole, and I can see you've had a terrible time."

I didn't know what to say. We were coming towards the exit gates, and there were security guards everywhere. One of the guards looked down at a notebook, and then back at the car.

"Get your head down," Dad said.

I did. He put his coat over my head, and slowed the car down to 5 mph, trying to avoid suspicion. But I knew the security guards were onto us. In the footwell, there was a map of Leisure World that must have been in there since we arrived. My spirits rose as I saw an area called "Pine Forest". The odds were long, but it was better than nothing. I looked up from behind the coat at the tops of the trees going by, the shady green light they made. I wasn't ready to leave. I put the map in my pocket and pushed open the door.

"Daniel!" Dad called. He made a grab for me but I was too quick for him. I rolled out onto the tarmac, and watched the car stop a few metres up the road. I got to my feet and bolted into the woods. I could hear Dad shouting as he scrambled out of the car, and the boots of the security guards as they joined the chase.

THIRTY-THREE

I knew I couldn't outrun the security guards. I couldn't even outrun Dad. But I also knew there were places they wouldn't be able – or willing – to follow. So I took the nastiest route, slashing my way through brambles and thorns. After ten minutes I found a steep dip in the land, and crouched down behind the ridge. I couldn't hear anyone following me. I'd lost them. I waited a moment and regained my breath before looking at the map again. "Pine Forest", it said. Maybe it was a big area, but at least all the pine was in one place. This narrowed it down significantly. I unfolded the map to its full size to see where the pine forest was. My heart sank. There were six other areas labelled "Pine Forest".

I kept moving, although my mood was low. I had to stay out of the reach of Dad and the authorities and it seemed that I was getting further and further away from Lexi, even though I hadn't got a clue where she was.

I stayed in the woods until nightfall. Every time I even approached one of the official paths, I saw Leisure World staff or security. My first step, if I was to have any chance of finding the place where Lexi woke, was to stay free. The problem was, I didn't have a second step.

Darkness fell early in the forest. Soon, I couldn't see ten metres. I sat down and rested. I was fitter than I'd ever been, but the exertion of the chase had still taken its toll. The spaces between the trees began to take on shapes. I was seeing things. At one point, I saw the burnt shapes of my mother and Dr Greggs, embracing. I started to think of where this hellish route had started. It looked like I was wrong: even if you had your time again, you couldn't change anything.

Two thuds and a metallic squeal ripped through the forest. "Two. Two. One, two, one, two," said a giant voice. Then the music began to play. They were making the final preparations for the Turn Back Time festival. I thought of Ryan and his friends in their wolf costumes and basketball vests. I had my second step.

THIRTY-FOUR

Fancy Stan's Dress Shop was understandably packed. Stan himself was dressed as a hippy, and he'd extended the opening hours because of the rush. Waiting in line, I couldn't help but look around for security guards. It seemed safe, but I made sure I tried on as many face masks as I could while I waited. I was everyone from Ronald McDonald to Margaret Thatcher.

Considering the hectic nature of his shop, Fancy Stan seemed very laid back. Perhaps he was taking his role as a hippy seriously. He looked down at me through his round purple spectacles. "What's your name, kid?" he said.

"Daniel."

"Good name, good name. Fancy Dan, I'm Fancy Stan. Good evening."

"Hi," I said.

Stan took a deep breath and waved his arms in the air. "Now. I'm going to read your mind. You're going to the festival and you want a costume. Something from the seventies, eighties or perhaps even the nineties."

"Yes, please," I said.

"I'm basically a clairvoyant," Fancy Stan said with a grin. "I'll be honest with you, kid. We're down to the dregs. All the cool seventies gear is gone, and we're out of Maradona wigs."

"I need something with a face mask," I said.

"Well, I wasn't going to say anything," Fancy Stan said. "But that's not a bad idea."

"What?" I said.

"Nothing. Nothing." He looked behind the counter, and picked up a tired old cardboard box. "I don't know what we've got for someone of your ... erm ... size. Ah, yes! This might do it."

He pulled out a Darth Vader helmet with a cloak. "That's perfect," I said.

"We haven't got the rest of the costume. We loaned it out to a stag party and the bloke threw up on it. It's at the dry cleaners."

"Doesn't matter," I said.

I pulled on the helmet and looked through the eyeholes at the mirror. I was wearing a blue hoody and jeans. It looked fairly strange but I was totally unrecognizable. Fancy Stan stood behind me.

"It's a wonder the Empire was ever defeated," he said. "Do you want a bag for that?"

"No," I said through the mask. "I'll keep it on."

The festival was crazy. For a company apparently so concerned with child welfare, it was surprising to see such a big bonfire in the same clearing as a sound stage. The fire cast a mad heat over the revellers. A tribute band called Guns N' Posers was playing on the stage, and the crowd was massive and garish. Big muscular men were done up as Baywatch babes, and every third person seemed to be dressed as Michael Jackson. Above the stage stood a gigantic clock. I was shocked to see its hands already pointing to twelve. A big cheer went up as midnight struck, and a guy in a Chewbacca costume walloped me on the back and laughed.

I was looking for Ryan. He knew Leisure World inside out, and I thought he might be able to tell me which of the pine forests were approachable by car, and if there was some kind of back entrance for vehicles. I figured that five guys dressed as basketball-playing wolves would be easy to find, but it was a strange kind of party.

As I made my way through the crowd, I noticed a group of security guards wading in. On the edges of the throng, I saw Evans directing the operation on his walkie-talkie. Dad was nowhere to be seen, and a part of me was disappointed. I wondered if he was looking for me elsewhere.

I tried to move away from the guards, but the crowd seemed to be closing around me. It was so hot inside the helmet, I was finding it difficult to breathe. The guards stopped a boy about a metre in front of me. He was dressed as a Scouser, with a curly black wig, but he was wearing a blue hoody to keep warm. It was just like mine.

"Take the wig off," the head security guard said.

"Why?" the Scouser said. "I haven't done anything."

The security guard slapped the Scouser across the head

and ripped off the wig. The boy fell to the ground.

"It's not him," the guard said, and the posse moved closer to where I stood. I realized they'd been told to look for a boy in a blue hoody, so I unzipped mine and let it slide off my arms to the ground. The guards were so close I could smell their sweat and aftershave.

"Hey, mate," said a guy dressed as a tin-foil Robocop. "You dropped this." He held out the hoody.

"No, I didn't," I said. I turned away. The security guard looked at me for a moment, but then the tribute band started up with "Welcome to the Jungle", someone screamed with excitement, and the guard was distracted.

It was a near miss, and – despairing of ever finding Ryan – I slinked out of the mass of people. The bonfire was in a clearing a few hundred metres from the main crowd, and I stood nearby for a moment, looking forlornly at the map.

Then I looked up, and the man was there.

For a moment I thought he was in costume. The long coat, the blood running down the neck, the angular hairstyle. He could've been from the eighties film *The Lost Boys*. I'd already seen a few people working that look. Absently he glanced over in my direction, and then he turned away. I'd almost forgotten I was wearing the mask. He didn't know who I was. I knew that Lexi had told me it wouldn't make any difference what I did to him, he'd still be there (wherever *there* was) when the clocks went back and struck one for the second time. But that hardly mattered. My first thought was just to hurt him. I picked up a sharp piece of wood that someone had tried to throw onto the bonfire. But then I calmed myself. Maybe if I followed him, he'd take me to where Lexi was, and I could be there for the extra hour.

But I kept the piece of wood, just in case.

I walked away, towards some trees where I would have cover to watch him. I could feel the chemical charge of excitement coursing through my body. When I was safely shaded by the trees, I took off the helmet. The heat of the bonfire had been overwhelming, and I needed to breathe.

Without the obstruction, I now had clear sight of the man. His arms were folded, and half of his coat shone slick in the firelight. I had never hated anyone so much in my life. I wondered why he hadn't just vanished, like Lexi. Luck, for once, was on my side, and if I could keep hold of my temper, there was a chance I could do something.

After a few minutes he began to walk. I kept close to the trees and followed. He was slinking about at the edge of the crowd, and it seemed to me that he was about to leave the event. He didn't rush, and he didn't seem to notice that I was following. I crept closer to him, away from the trees. Even the way he moved was sickening, like a fly crawling on your food. I knew he might turn around at any moment, so I put down the piece of wood, to put my mask back on.

That's when they found me. Jack, Thorpey and Lewis, the boys from the swimming pool. They were dressed as the Ghostbusters.

"Look who it is. Darth Fat-boy," said Thorpey.

"That's not very good, Thorpey," said Jack. He turned to

me. I could see a hint of fear in his eyes, the memory of the invisible force that had pulled him into the water. "We've been looking for you, Dan," he said.

I glanced over to where I'd last seen the man, but he was gone. He couldn't have got far, but I needed to work fast if I was to find him again. "Just give me a couple of hours, OK? Then you can do what you want with me."

Thorpey and Lewis laughed. Jack shook his head. "You're not in any position to call the shots. You belong to us. And there'll be none of your water tricks this time."

"I don't need water to do that," I said.

He stared at me for moment. "You're bluffing," he said.

I dropped the helmet and reached down for the piece of wood, but Lewis got there first. He took a swipe at me, but missed. I turned, and ran towards the trees. I had my keys in my pocket. Dad had shown me how to carry my keys between my fingers and use them as a weapon if I felt under threat. I searched through my pockets now. Lewis caught me and kicked my legs away. I fell, with my hands in my pockets, unable to break the impact. My chin snapped forward and smacked the ground. I was out cold.

SUNDAY 28 OCTOBER

THIRTY-FIVE

The first thing I saw when I woke was the huge clock above the stage. It was one thirty. For a moment, I panicked. Had the clocks been turned back already? Was it one thirty for the *second* time? Had I been unconscious that long? No. On stage, the master of ceremonies was geeing up the crowd. "It's half one, ladies and gentleman, so the clocks go back in half an hour. It's just more time to rock! Our next act is a bit special. All the way from Dublin, it's Ireland's very best Michael Jackson tribute band ... *Triller!*" A huge cheer went up.

So I'd only been out for fifteen minutes, but it didn't make much difference. The man was gone, and I'd never find him now. The idiot boys had stolen my map. I had half an hour until Lexi woke, seven possible pine forests to cover, and no one to follow. I had no energy, and no hope. It was all over.

The noise of the crowd was too much for me. I wanted to be alone, so I walked out past the bonfire, into the dark woods, and out to the lake. I went to the clearing where Lexi had set up camp, and I sat by the water for a while. *Perhaps they'll never find me*, I thought. *Maybe I'll just stay here until Monday, so I can see her again.* But I knew that wasn't going to happen.

I bent down and put my face into the water. It was grainy and cold, welcome against my sore skin. I breathed out slowly, felt the air leave my lungs. I felt like staying underwater until I passed out. But there, at the end of my breath, was a vision. It wasn't Lexi in the Dome, or Lexi sitting in the tree, or Lexi in her makeshift Indian headdress. In fact, it wasn't Lexi at all. It was Chrissy. She was kneeling behind me with her hands over my eyes, as she had done that day at the volleyball court. *"Our lives,"* she said, as she had said back then. *"Our lives are written on our bodies."*

I raised my head from the water, sucked in a deep breath, and thought about those words. Then the flashbacks came to me: Lexi's body, as it was moments before she disappeared in the steam room. The cuts on her legs were like icicles, and they were sparkling. They were sparkling with sandy red dust. The grains had shimmered and glinted when she moved. There was only one place in Leisure World with red dust: the all-weather pitches. As the realization hit home my whole body convulsed with pain. The gash on my leg returned, my ankle expanded with swelling, and I felt the gouge in my side open up, the blood weeping. My trainers and my legs were covered in sandy red dust.

I looked down at my watch. The minute hand ticked backwards one stroke.

* * *

I came out of the forest by a bike stand. By the law of averages, I knew one of the bikes had to be unlocked. I pulled at the mountain bikes and the BMXs, but the first one to come away from its mooring was a Shopper. I didn't have time to worry about looks. I cycled onwards, slowly, painfully, the wounds making every metre agony.

I stared down at my injuries with wonder. They were my future. I knew, at least, that I would make it to the forest. But I didn't know if I would be too late to save Lexi. And I didn't know if I would survive those wounds.

As I neared the all-weather pitch, all I could see was the whites of the goalposts. The floodlights, of course, had been turned off. I was freezing cold, and the pain was too much, now. I couldn't cycle in a straight line, and eventually I fell off the bike and lay on the ground. I was exhausted. The wheel of the Shopper skated around, the dynamo clicked and the bike light flickered and then went out. All I could hear was the sound of my own breathing and the muffled chant of the festival crowd, counting down: "Five, four, three, two, one..."

The power surged through me, and I scrambled to my feet. The wounds were gone and my watch began to tick forward. It was one o'clock, again. I sprinted towards the all-weather pitches. The extra hour had begun.

THIRTY-SIX

I saw the man before I saw Lexi. He was standing at the edge of the all-weather pitch, and his frosted breath was spiralling into the air. The temperature had suddenly plummeted, and I could see an icy sheen on the bark of the trees; the whole place was tingling with cold. *The big freeze*, I thought. *Of course.*

The man hurled a pair of keys into the forest, wiped his hands and walked around the outside of the playing surface, keeping to the grass so his footprints wouldn't show up in the red sand. I reached the complex just as he pulled a pen-torch out of his pocket and shone it at Lexi. She was lying on the pitch, wearing the blue dress and black leggings I'd read about in the newspaper article. She raised her hand to shield her eyes from the light. He walked over, took her by the hair and the arms and dragged her towards the pine forest. I thought of the welts on her scalp. I was a hundred metres away. Maybe more. Had I arrived a few minutes earlier things could have been different.

I called out. "Lexi!"

My voice echoed back from the surfaces of that strange cold plain. The natural and the artificial.

As he reached the trees, he turned and looked at me.

His movements quickened; he picked her up and put her over his shoulder, and soon they were in the trees, out of sight, but already I felt powerful as I ran towards them across the red gravel. Lexi had told me that the actions of that hour played out the same every time, that she was powerless to change them. But I had changed them already. I had made the man turn around.

By the time I got to the first pines, there was no sign of them. I called her name again.

"I'm coming," I said. I kept running, but then I stopped, listening for the sound of footsteps crunching on the frozen ground. I thought I heard the sound of breaking twigs to my left, so I turned and ran in that direction.

I was right. Up ahead in the dark, their movements were hard to distinguish. I could see that she was struggling on the ground, and he was kneeling over her, ripping at her clothes. I thought I saw the punch that caused her black eye.

I increased my speed, but tripped on a root. I felt my ankle turn over. Sprained at least. It was the strangest feeling, because I had seen the damage before. I got up and limped on.

"Stop," I tried to shout, but I was so tired, so cold, that I barely made a sound. I knew what was coming. He pulled off her leggings, but as he did so, she kicked him and stood. I was close enough to see the desperation on her face. This was the moment she had talked about, when she escaped him for a few seconds, but she wasn't fast enough to get away. *Go, Lexi,* I thought. *Go faster.*

But she didn't. She stopped. She had seen me, and the future was changing. It seemed to take her a moment to recognize me. "Daniel? No. Go away. Get out of here, please!"

"Run, Lexi!" I said.

She looked at me and then at the man, who was groggily rising to his knees. And she ran.

I got to him a few seconds later and thrust a knee into his face. He fell back, but he pulled me down with him. I didn't see him reach for the knife, but I felt him lunge at me. I rolled away and the knife slid down my shin, opening that familiar gash. I screamed, and flung out a fist, catching him in the mouth. We wrestled, but his strength was awesome. He pinned my arms with his knees, leaving his knife hand free. Lexi was right. He was too strong.

I felt his breath on me, as Lexi had felt it. The stinging mint and the whiskey behind it. His face looked pale in the moonlight, his lips full. I noticed the length of his eyelashes as he stared down at me.

"I wouldn't want to be you," I said.

He frowned, and lifted the knife. *She must have got away,* I thought. *I've saved her.* He sunk the knife into my stomach, and I felt the red hot pain deep in my gut. For a moment, it didn't seem to matter, but then I saw that Lexi had returned. She was metres away. She came back because she cared about me. We cared about each other, and that – it seemed – was our downfall.

"Daniel, no!" she screamed. He pulled out the knife and turned, got to his feet and left me behind. He was gaining on her before they were even out of my sight. I knew he was bound to catch her.

I was in a bad way; there was a metallic taste in my mouth, and I could barely feel my legs. The cold from the ground crept into my skin. But the adrenalin had kicked in and I was able to stand. I limped deeper into the woods. I could hear them up ahead, hear her breathing and the cries of panic between. *I'm going to see it*, I thought. *I'm going to see him kill her.* I couldn't bear that. I heard a sudden swipe and crack, and the sound of a body hitting the ground. I felt the force of the blow echoing through the woods. There was no more panic in me, just a huge sadness; a sad acceptance that this was what men were like. I ran in the direction of the sound. Soon, through the trees I could see a dark figure standing with a body at his feet. I kept running towards him, this standing figure. It was my father.

THIRTY-SEVEN

I had prior experience of hallucinations, of course. And that was when I *didn't* have a hole in my stomach. But there was no doubt that this was my dad. I knew the shape of him even in the dark. As I staggered closer, his features became clear. He was holding a seven-iron golf club, and the man lay writhing at his feet. "Daniel?" he said.

"What are you *doing* here?" I said.

I could see that he was shaking. He looked down at the man. "I was looking for you, Daniel. But then this guy comes bolting out of nowhere, chasing the—"

"Where is she?" I shouted.

"Who? The girl?"

"Where is she?" I was screaming, delirious, spinning around looking for Lexi.

"She ran off. Look, she's OK. *He's* not going anywhere, is he?" Dad said, pointing to the man, who was flat out now. Twitching slightly. A sticky blackness in his hair. It was too dark for Dad to see my wounds. "Why is it so bloody *cold*?" he said.

I didn't answer. I heard rustling in the woods and I set off after the sound. "Daniel, come back, for God's sake!" Dad said.

"I've got to go," I said, but then I stopped and turned. "How can *you* see them?"

"You what?"

"How could you see them? Him. And Lexi."

"Well," he said. "The moon's quite strong, and you soon get used to the dark."

"No, I mean..." I thought of what Lexi had said, about a special sensitivity. About good *mindsight. Surely not*, I thought. "Forget it," I said. "Just stay there. With him." There would be time for questions later.

"Daniel, wait," Dad said. But I didn't wait. I ran.

I was crying, but I didn't know what the emotion was. I'd never felt it before. I looked down at my watch. It was one forty-seven. I was getting weaker, but I didn't care. Soon enough I could see her up ahead, leaping over the stumps and the ferns, dodging between the tree trunks, her blue dress shimmering. I tried to call her name, but I couldn't get the breath to do it.

She was laughing. I chased her as I had done that night when we jumped the fences. And, like that night, I never caught up.

A few minutes later, we left the pine forest, and were surrounded by beeches and oaks, the ancient trees of the old forest. We circled the lake and eventually I arrived at the clearing I had come to know so well.

When I got there, she was nowhere to be seen. I looked around at the burnt-out cooking pit, and the red sand that had fallen from my shoes before.

"Lexi!" I called. I looked up, and saw her in the tree, walking carefully, arms out, along the solid branch which overhung the water. She turned to me.

"Thank you, Danny-boy," she said.

She sprang from the branch and sliced through the surface of the water, almost without a sound. I watched for a moment, but when she didn't reappear, I dived in after her. For a few moments everything was dark and swirling with loose soil. I fought to keep the rank water out of my nose and mouth, and then I began to settle. The old rhythm returned. I felt my body sinking. One, and. Two, and. Three, and.

I opened my eyes, and I knew I was deep. The water was luminous, and green. Blood corkscrewed up from the wound in my stomach, like smoke. The blood looked dark and slick in the green water.

I could see her. She was far deeper than me, far deeper than I believed the lake to be. She sculled with long, slow strokes down towards the bottom, where the light was changing colour. Eventually, as I got closer, I could see the source of the coloured light: it was Lexi's front door, sunk into the earth. She was moving through the beams of luminous water, towards it. I could see the shadows of figures behind the glass; the red glass and the blue.

I couldn't go any deeper. My breath was almost gone. I stopped swimming, and allowed the water to pull me up. When I broke the surface, I could hear the giant clock smacking out the hour. It was, finally, 2 a.m.

THIRTY-EIGHT

The frost was gone from the forest floor. Dad was close to where I had left him, but he looked scared.

"Daniel, you must stay with me, now, OK? I can't have you running off again."

He took me by the shoulders, and examined me. "What's that?" he said, looking down at my bloodstained T-shirt. "Are you cut? Did he cut you?"

"No," I said. I lifted the T-shirt to reveal the smooth, unblemished skin beneath. All the wounds were gone, and I knew they were gone for good. "It must be his blood, or something."

"Where's the lass?" he said.

"Couldn't find her," I said.

"There's something weird going off here. What aren't you telling me?"

"Nothing. It's—"

"That fella I hit," Dad said. He looked disturbed, afraid to say it. "He's *gone*."

I nodded.

"No, Daniel. You don't understand. He didn't get up and run off. He just, well. It's stupid. He just..."

"Vanished."

"Aye," Dad said. He glanced about him at the stern uniformity of the pine trunks. "I tell you what. I'm not happy with this. I'm not happy with this, at all."

"Did he disappear around two o'clock? When the gongs sounded, over at the festival?" I asked.

"Dead on," Dad said.

"Dead on," I said quietly. "Listen, Dad. It's best if you don't mention any of this to the people from Leisure World."

"It's too late. I've already called them."

I was tired of running away, and it didn't matter to me what some fool from a holiday camp said about my mental health. Dad was a bit more wary of speaking to the officials now, after what he had done, but I think part of him just wanted to get back to civilization. We saw the white beams of their torches raking the forest well before we emerged onto the all-weather pitches. The Leisure World vans were soon joined by a couple of police cars, and we were taken into a small room in the huge administrative building. It was a strange place to be at 2.30 a.m., the ghostly emptiness of an office at night.

While the police put out search teams for a missing girl and an injured man, we were questioned by Officer Bracket, a tall, straight-backed woman from the local force, and the ridiculous Evans. I didn't speak. I didn't give them Lexi's name.

I pretended to be in shock. Even after the violence of the last few hours, I felt so peaceful, imagining Lexi diving towards the glass in the door. Dad, however, couldn't hold his mouth.

"I'm just telling you what happened," he said.

Officer Bracket nodded and scribbled in her notepad. "And how did you know that your son would be in the pine forest?"

"It's down by the football pitches, isn't it? He's a big fan of football."

I stared at Dad, but he wouldn't meet my eye.

"This is all nonsense," Evans said. "Safety and security is our number one concern here, and there's no way we'd allow this ... *man* you speak of onto our premises." He turned to Officer Bracket. "I wouldn't trust anything Mr Lever says. He's been drunk for most of his time here at Leisure World. He has obstructed our attempts to secure the safety of his son, of whom he has been neglectful. And he has abused our staff, including me—"

"That's because you're a tosser," Dad said. "And if you don't shut up, I'll—"

"Gentlemen, *please*," Officer Bracket said. "You both need to cool down. Mr Evans, you and I are going to go out into the corridor and have a little chat. Mr Lever, you and Daniel keep each other company in here for a moment."

Evans exited with Officer Bracket, and Dad sighed. "I just feel like poking the little swine in the eye," he said. "But I won't."

For a moment there was silence in the room.

"Dad," I said.

"Yes."

"A big fan of football?"

He smiled. "Aye. I hope they don't give you a ball and ask you to prove it."

"Leisure World is massive, Dad. It can't have been a coincidence that we ran into each other. How did you *really* know I'd be there?"

"Your girlfriend told me."

"What?"

"That lass. She came up to me outside the cabin the other night. After you and me had argued about ... you know, Tash. She's a strange girl, Daniel. She was wearing a big red coat and she had her hood up so I could hardly see her face."

I thought back to that night, the flash of red I had seen moving towards our cabin. The last time she'd worn the coat. Lexi had been late to meet me, I should have guessed.

Dad continued with a frown. "She nearly scared me to death. I was having a fag. Don't tell your mother."

"What did she say?"

"Said you might be about to do something stupid on Saturday night. Told me to look for you down by the all-weather pitches."

"And you didn't talk to me about it?" I said.

"I thought she was talking nonsense. A young lass comes up to you like that, starts spouting on... Well, I never gave it a moment's thought until you went missing. I figured it must be the place where you and her hung around."

"So why didn't you tell that to the police?"

"Didn't want to get the two of you into trouble. I couldn't

tell *them* you were going to do something stupid, could I?"

My head was spinning.

"I've got some questions of my own, Daniel," Dad said.

"Maybe we should talk about it later," I said.

Dad whistled and shook his head. "Well. I don't really understand what happened out there tonight," he said. "First it was freezing cold, then it suddenly gets warmer. And that fella! I hit him pretty hard, but I just can't account for where he went. I don't even know if I *killed* the poor bugger."

"You shouldn't have any sympathy for him, Dad," I said. I paused, but I had to say it, because it was true. "You did the right thing."

A few moments later, Officer Bracket came back in with Evans and an unexpected guest: my mum. She came straight over and threw her arms around me. She was wearing her blue woollen coat, and the smell of it made me cry. "You OK?" she asked.

I nodded.

She turned to Dad. "Are you?" she said.

"Oh aye," he said. "Not a scratch."

"Thanks for calling me," Mum said to him.

Evans marched over. "Mrs Lever," he said, in his old patronizing voice. "I think it would be best for you and your family if this whole embarrassing mess was wrapped up as soon as possible."

"It's not embarrassing for us, Mr Evans. How about I call the press, and then we'll see for whom it's embarrassing," Mum said. She stood and turned around. "Let's talk to the national papers about invasion of privacy, and you masquerading as some sort of social worker."

"Your boy has damaged our property. He threw stones at a security camera."

"A *concealed* security camera," Mum said. "What else are you hiding, Mr Evans?"

"I'm not hiding anything. Your husband – sorry, your *estranged* husband – is making up ludicrous stories about young girls being attacked in forests. I will not have Leisure World's good name dragged through the mud again."

"Again?" Mum said.

Evans looked away.

Beeps and static hissed through Officer Bracket's radio. "Receiving," she said, and walked off to a corner of the room. It wasn't long before she returned. "They've found two bodies," she said.

Evans smashed his fist against the wall, and Dad held his head in his hands. "Oh my God," he said. "I killed that fella."

"You didn't kill anybody," Officer Bracket said. "These bodies were badly decomposed. Early signs indicate that they've been in the forest for two years."

"What?" Dad said. He looked at me and I met his stare. The reality of her body, out there in the forest, hit me hard. I put my hands over my eyes and tried to imagine what Lexi would say. She'd tell me that she'd left her body a long time ago, that it was just dead cells. Just matter.

"Daniel, are you OK?" Mum asked.

"I will be," I said.

*   *   *

The police would still need to talk to us, they said. They'd need to talk to Evans, too. In the corridor I heard Mum calmly telling Officer Bracket that my father's statement had been confused due to his mental state: his son was missing, and he was enduring a difficult divorce. She said he'd probably just found the body and gone into shock.

Dad came out of the toilets a moment later and Mum stopped talking. We walked, the three of us, out to the car park. The sun was coming up, and the birds were calling. In the car park Mum kissed me and told me she would see me soon.

"Do you want to come back in the car with us?" Dad asked.

Mum smiled. "Richard. I've got my own car. I can't just leave it here," she said.

"No. I suppose not."

She put a hand on his arm and then let it fall. I got into the car with Dad, and we watched Mum drive away. Then we followed.

The twisted trunks of the trees went by my window like the letters and words of a language I didn't know. Incomprehensible, yet reassuring. Through the gaps, I occasionally saw the flashing light of a police car. We passed the glistening lake, the Pancake House, the noble Dome.

I twisted in my seat to make sure Dad had brought all my bags. On the back shelf stood the cherry tomato plant, its fruit huge and red and bursting with life.

I found it hard to watch the news channels as the information came in. Her name was on the banners that scrolled across the bottom of the TV screen. The story filtered through over the next few weeks and months.

The body of Alexandria Cocker was found in a covered ditch in the pine forest, close to that of Marcus Fielding, 34. Fielding had worked in the bookings department of Leisure World, but had left without notice. Guests had made several complaints about his behaviour towards young women, all of which had been ignored by the Leisure World management. The torched wreckage of a stolen sports car found on the site around the time of the murder was thought to be the car he had used. At the time, the car's theft had been attributed to local vandals.

The girl in the news articles was not really the Lexi I knew and loved, and it made me strangely angry. *You don't know her*, I thought, when I saw her school-friends – most of them at university now – talking about her. It wasn't that they said she was better or worse than she was; just different. Experience changes people, of course. I know it has changed me.

I couldn't eat the tomatoes from the plant, and Dad only ate a few. I much preferred to watch them grow, checking every day that their progress had not reversed. It never did, and Dad began to neglect the plant, leaving it out in the cold garden. I have never watched anything rot with such relief and glee. The shrivelling, blackening, exploding mess was beautiful to me.

Dad, of course, was much more disturbed by the news coverage. He had spoken to a girl on the lawn of his holiday cabin a few days before, seen her running through a pine forest, and now the TV was telling him she'd been dead for two years. Credit to him, he didn't angrily try to explain it away, as I thought he would. And he didn't blame me. If he'd have asked, I'd have told him everything, but he didn't.

He went to see a psychotherapist Chrissy had recommended. I don't know if he talked about what he had seen at Leisure World, but I suspect he talked about Mum and about me. He's getting better. One step at a time. He bought a new TV, but it still links up to the security camera. We can't seem to disconnect it.

I went back to school as soon as I could. I don't know if I behaved any differently, but you don't ask the fat kid (or even the "slightly-thinner-than-before kid') if he had a holiday romance when he was suspended from school. I settled back in. I swam a lot.

For a while, I felt pretty sad, and it seemed that every time I started to feel better, another one of those news item came up. There was something in the paper about a possible charge against Evans for obstructing the course of justice, or a piece of evidence linking Marcus Fielding to another crime. But in the February after we returned from Leisure World, BBC news interviewed Lexi's dad, Paul Cocker, outside his house. He was talking about starting a charity in Lexi's name. I wasn't really listening, because I was staring past him, at his other daughter. Lexi was right, she was a beauty, and behind her was the glass door, the sails of the ship coated in frost on that cold morning. I thought, briefly, about going there, to the house. I was pretty sure I could find it. But in the end I didn't go. I couldn't. Not without her permission.

In March, the clocks went forward and we lost an hour. *Good riddance to it*, I thought.

Around that time, I was watching a documentary about the massacre at Wounded Knee, and I noticed a mark on the TV. I squinted hard, but it was difficult to make out. I switched the TV off and crouched down in front of the set. Burnt shapes began to emerge. For a moment, I thought Dad had used the security camera to check who was downstairs. I actually thought the person whose orange shape I could see on the glass was me. But it wasn't. It was a girl, with her arms folded. She seemed to be wearing a feather in her hair.

After that, every once in a while, I would be standing in a crowd, or waiting in line for the bus, and I would feel a little tap on my shoulder. I would spin around and sense someone running away. It's called a coup, and it's a brave and difficult thing – to touch someone, and then let them go.

Edward Hogan was born in Derby in 1980 and lives in Brighton. His first adult novel, *Blackmoor*, won the Desmond Elliot Prize and was shortlisted for the Sunday Times Young Writer of the Year Award and the Dylan Thomas Prize. *Daylight Saving* is his first novel for teenagers.

About *Daylight Saving,* Ed says, "When I was about twelve, I visited a sports holiday camp, and really enjoyed it. My brother and I loved sport, and there was something powerfully haunting about the fact that this place was set in an ancient forest. Thousand-year-old trees stood next to pizza restaurants and floodlit tennis courts. I was interested in this old/new clash. I also thought that if you didn't like sport (and Daniel, the narrator of *Daylight Saving*, doesn't), it could be a very lonely place indeed.

"*Daylight Saving* is a ghost story, but it's also a story about family, and a story about two independent young people, Daniel and Lexi. I'd been thinking a lot about trauma when I wrote the book. When something bad happens to you, it can feel like time has sort of stopped, that you're trapped in the past. That's what's happened to Lexi, really. She is stuck in the loop of her terrible experience, while Daniel feels responsible for the breakdown of his family. It is only through their relationship that they can understand the things that have happened to them, and know that it's possible to have love without rage, and desire without destruction; that a traumatic incident doesn't have to own your soul; that while grief can't be ignored, it is possible – with a little gentleness, and a little help – to reclaim yourself."

UNDER COVER

READ BETWEEN THE LINES

 READ
- Sneak previews
- Author interviews

DISCOVER
- Trailers
- Behind the scenes footage

 WIN
- Review copies
- Signed books

COMMENT

Have your say on the books that you want to read

Scan the code to watch our book trailers*

Discover more at
WWW.UNDERCOVERREADS.COM